James Grant

Lady Wedderburn's Wish

Vol. III: A Tale of the Crimean War

James Grant

Lady Wedderburn's Wish
Vol. III: A Tale of the Crimean War

ISBN/EAN: 9783743418479

Manufactured in Europe, USA, Canada, Australia, Japa

Cover: Foto ©Andreas Hilbeck / pixelio.de

Manufactured and distributed by brebook publishing software (www.brebook.com)

James Grant

Lady Wedderburn's Wish

LADY WEDDERBURN'S WISH.

A Tale of the Crimean War.

By JAMES GRANT,

AUTHOR OF "THE ROMANCE OF WAR," "FIRST LOVE AND LAST LOVE,"
"THE GIRL HE MARRIED," ETC.

IN THREE VOLUMES.

VOL. III.

LONDON:

TINSLEY BROTHERS, 18, CATHERINE STREET, STRAND.
1870.

CONTENTS

OF

THE THIRD VOLUME.

—

CHAP.		PAGE
I.	LE RESTAURANT DE L'ARMÉE D'ORIENT	1
II.	THE DUEL À MORT	10
III.	THE ALMA	30
IV.	THE 21st OF SEPTEMBER	45
V.	WOUNDED AND MISSING	58
VI.	THE WINTER OF THE YEAR	65
VII.	SCUTARI	76
VIII.	HOW IT CAME TO PASS	85
IX.	THE NIGHT MARCH TO TCHORGOUN	93
X.	A PRISONER OF WAR	109
XI.	THE PAROLE OF HONOUR	125
XII.	THE YACHT	138

vi CONTENTS.

CHAP.		PAGE
XIII.	FATE	149
XIV.	THE CITY OF THE SILENT	157
XV.	DREAMS REALIZED	167
XVI.	TEA WITH MADAME TEGOBORSKI	184
XVII.	GALITZIN AS A LOVER	194
XVIII.	THE PROGRESS HE MADE	203
XIX.	HORACE'S PLEASANT TASK	217
XX.	GWENNY'S PLAN	227
XXI.	A NEW FRIEND	241
XXII.	THE LOST PATH	252
XXIII.	PERA	260
XXIV.	THE CAVE OF FOUL KOUBA	266
XXV.	CONCLUSION	275

LADY WEDDERBURN'S WISH.

CHAPTER I.

LE RESTAURANT DE L'ARMÉE D'ORIENT.

"We are going to have cigars and a bottle of Greek wine," said Cyril to the Zouave Captain, who seemed at first doubtful about entering, and then acceded with a bow. Cyril thought that perhaps he was a man of high French family and did not care much to mix with the *sous-officiers*, many of whom were then mingling with their superiors, playing chess or dominoes, laughing, smoking, chatting gaily, or perusing the *Charivari;* even *Punch* and the *Illustrated News*, which were not wanting for the amusement of the British officers, many of whom were in the large and strange-looking coffee-room, which had been the place where the horses and camels had been stabled when the house was a khan of high repute. On many parts of the walls were coloured prints of Parisian girls, opera and ballet dancers,

1

pirouetting in the shortest of drapery, and round them the Turks were wont to gather in amazement, and to mutter that such beauties were worthy of the Padisha himself.

Everything that he saw filled Horace, like every new comer, with wonder, or excited his interest; strange dresses, manners, voices and faces; but Cyril had already become intimate with all these as if he had known them from boyhood.

He who arrives in any place which is to be his quarters for a time, feels as if the strange streets, the public edifices, the churches, and the sound of their bells, would never become familiar; yet Horace was so much of a soldier that he had not been three days in and about Varna before the aspect of the itinerant Dervises, who received his piastres or paras with a malediction; the shrill invitation of the Muezzin from the minaret; the Turk kneeling at prayer on a bit of tattered carpet in the open street, counting his *colomboio*, and scowling with horror at the passing Highlander; the French *vivandière* riding at the head of a battalion of Chasseurs à Cheval, and waggishly kissing her hand to some fat old Pasha; the women stealing along like sheeted spectres in their white yashmacs and yellow boots; the jolly gangs of British tars, trundling up their Lancaster guns from the beach like toys, became all familiar, for the sense of novelty was gone.

They had scarcely entered before several of

their brother-officers came forward from amid the various tables and groups to accost them, for the cousins were decidedly popular among the Fusileers. There were Bingham, Jack Probyn, old Conyers Singleton the Major, and Pat Beamish, with his black whiskers more bushy than ever.

"Welcome to Varna, Horace, though bad luck to it for a hole, anyhow!" said Beamish; "for if we don't get out of it sharp, between raki and unripe fruit, we'll leave half our men behind us."

"Orders and advice go for nothing, so far as these are concerned," added the Major.

"Bedad, the arms of Briareus and the eyes of Argus wont keep these Greek devils with their fruit out of the camp; and there's Bingham of ours narrowly escaped a slash from a yataghan for peeping through the holes of a woman's yashmac in a sherbet shop yesterday, and giving her a chuck under the chin."

"Is that Home of the Guards with a cocked hat?" asked Horace, as he saw the Master of Ernescleugh seated jauntily on a table, laughing with some French and Turkish officers.

"Yes; he's on the staff."

"An aide-de-camp?"

"Yes, and enjoys the fullest confidence of the General," said Beamish; "but here, unfortunately, he cannot have that which is so indispensable to the position of an aide-de-camp—the confidence of the General's wife and daughters."

Colonel De la Fosse, who was seated at a table with a few officers of the French 34th, now rose and lifted his cap to Horace, who said—

"Allow me, Colonel, to introduce my brother officer, Captain Wedderburn. It was De la Fosse," he added to Cyril, "who in some measure revenged you on Chesters; but, by the way, in the troop-ship we agreed not to refer to that subject."

"Ah, now, comrade, it was to your kind father I believe that I owe the favour of being what I now am," said the Colonel, as he warmly shook Cyril's hand; "for his opportune assistance saved me, when yonder brigand put me in a sore strait indeed!"

Wine and cigars were speedily brought, and the new arrivals proceeded through their medium to enjoy the buzz and heedless merriment around them. The restaurant was soon densely crowded, and the mixture of languages, French, English, Turkish, Greek, and often a polyglot of them all, and bad Bulgarian, were heard on all sides. The only silent person was the observant Captain of Zouaves who accompanied Cyril and Horace, and who, oddly enough, seemed far from being at ease

"Drink with us, Monsieur," said Colonel De la Fosse. "You are very silent for a Zouave; your fellows have the reputation of being more noisy than even the Tourlourous," he added, laughing, as he used the sobriquet for the French Linesmen.

"I am thinking of Paris," replied the Captain. "But we must rough it as best we may, for potages and jellies, ragoûts, and pâtés are all unknown here."

"But you can have kidneys fried in champagne," said Beamish; "or claret mulled with a dash of clove or a slice of pineapple, and sure these are luxuries enough for any man on service."

"Yes; but here one longs for the cafés chantants, the theatres, the casinos, and the girls of Paris, with their sparkling black eyes and white shoulders."

"*Ah, ces épaules blanches !*" said a sous-lieutenant, throwing up his eyes. "True; for the women here look hideous in their shapeless mufflings."

"Your regiment, mon Capitaine, is the——" De la Fosse paused and twirled his moustache.

"The 1st Zouaves, mon Colonel," replied the other, curtly.

"Ah, encamped at present a mile or two beyond the Devna Lake."

"Exactly, Monsieur," replied the Zouave Captain, who seemed to dislike the expression of scrutiny he read in the keen eyes of the Colonel, who wore the square peak of his scarlet kepi close to his nose.

" It was your regiment that led the van at
the Pass of Djerma ?"

" Yes, Monsieur," replied the Zouave, while
the Colonel tugged at his moustache more than
ever.

" I too am sick of Varna," said a gay-looking
Chasseur à Cheval, " and long, if not for active
service, for the pleasures of Paris; a ramble in
the Place de la Concorde, or the Gardens of the
Tuileries, or to take my ease in the Hôtel de
Lausanne, instead of the devilish old tumbledown Restaurant de l'Armée d'Orient."

" Yes; and perhaps to run after the nurses
and grisettes," said the Zouave Captain.

" Tra la la la, l'amour est là !" sang the
Chasseur. " Well, perhaps, yes."

" But," said Cyril, " there are no grisettes
such as we find in the romances of Paul de Koch
and his predecessor, the author of the ' Con-
quests of Mademoiselle Zina' (over which the
Emperor slept on the retreat from Leipzig)—
the grisette is now a *petite dame.*"

" Any way you take it," replied the Zouave,
with a growing irritation of manner. " We have
but a dreary time of it here, nursing the sick
and burying the dead; no fighting, no glory;
patience—always patience. *Mal peste !* what we
have endured since our troops came down the
passes of the Balkan !"

" Your reward is at hand, Monsieur," said De

la Fosse.   "In four days we leave this to attack the enemy !"

A burst of applause followed this announcement, and hearty English cheers, mingled with shrill yells of *"Vive la France!"* *"Vive l'Empereur!"* the old cry that rang over Waterloo, and many a field of the past !

"In what direction is the attack ?" asked the Zouave, eagerly.

"I am not yet at liberty to say."

"But your authority is undoubted, Monsieur ?"

"I had it from Marshal St. Arnaud himself."

"I am glad to hear of it," added the Zouave. "Gunpowder is the incense amid which the souls of the brave go straight to God."

"Somehow, that bit of bombast is the only thing this fellow has said like a true Frenchman," whispered Cyril to Horace.

"In four days," exclaimed the young chasseur. *"Ouf, ma foi!"* we'll eat the Muscovites up— train oil, tallow, and all the rest of it !"

"And now, Messieurs, adieu," said the Zouave, as he drained his wineglass, put his sword under his arm, and with a low bow quitted the café. The keen glance of De la Fosse followed him, and then fell on Cyril Wedderburn. Each read doubt in the other's eye.

"Is that Captain of Zouaves much about the camp ?" he asked.

"Daily; but he keeps more among the British than the Turks."

"I am sorry to hear this."

"Why, Monsieur?" asked Cyril.

"Because it adds to my suspicions," said De la Fosse, lowering his voice. "He showed a purse with more gold in it than usually falls to the lot of a captain of Zouaves; and he spoke of the First leading the van at Djerma, when it was *I* who led the van there, at the head of the 3rd Zouaves, and 3rd Chasseurs à Pied."

"Do you mean to say that you think——"

"I know not what to think; but fear to be rash. To detain him, might excite a bad feeling between the Zouaves and ours, if he be innocent; but anyway, I shall ride to Devna to-morrow, and see his regiment on parade."

"You had not many scruples about unmasking our Major of the Turkish Contingent," said Horace, laughing.

"Ah! but then I knew him of old," replied the Colonel; "and I detected his false play while watching, with regret, a signet ring he wore; an onyx graven with my crest, a gauntlet on the point of a sword, with the motto, *Droit en avant* —a ring that had been long in my family, and which we valued highly, because there is a terrible story attached to it. He won it from me, however, at play, when I madly staked and was stripped of everything."

" And what is this story, if I may inquire?"
asked Wedderburn.

" It belongs to the old days when duelling
was alike a passion and a vice with the French,
who carried it almost to a pitch of insanity ; and
if it wile a little of this time, which we find so
irksome in Varna, I care not if I relate to you
the affair, as illustrative of the days of our grand-
fathers—in France at least."

" *Bon ! très bon !* Agreed! Very good! Fire
away ! Colonel," said several voices in French
and English ; and after more wine and cigars
had been brought, the Colonel related the following story.

CHAPTER II.

THE DUEL À MORT.

"Louis XV. of France, died in 1765. It was in the year preceding that event that my grand-uncle, Louis De la Fosse, whose ring that man Chesters now wears, fought the famous duel I am about to relate to you; but prior to doing this, I must go a little way back into the history of himself, and that of the time, now some ninety years ago.

"My family is of Languedoc, and for several generations we have resided near Montpellier; thus it chanced that when my great-uncle Louis was a student attending the Royal College there, he became acquainted with a youth named Renée de Taillevant De l'Isle, from Provence, and a friendship sprung up between them. The circumstance of Louis' only sister Henriette, a beautiful blonde, being not indisposed to view the handsome Renée—for Renée was so—with favour, conduced greatly to cement this regard; and at the house of Louis most of the spare time of Renée was spent, when studies were over.

"Both lads were destined for the army; every gentleman of good family in France took a turn of military service, then in some fashion, with the Mousquetaires, the Line, or as a volunteer; and knowing that the time would come when they should be inexorably separated, their friendship, the spontaneous growth of two generous and affectionate hearts, of similarity of taste and thought, was all the stronger.

"They had gone through the same classes at college; they practised together the use of the sword, and soon taught each other to excel all their companions in every trick of the science of self-defence. They hunted together in the mountains, boated together on the Rhone, and accompanied by Henriette, had many a wild gallop among the beautiful groves of olive and mulberry trees, which grow there in much luxuriance, for Languedoc is one of France's most favoured regions; and on these occasions the fair Henriette, with her golden hair dressed *à la Marquise*, looked like a beauty by Watteau, in her riding-habit of *gris-de-lin*, then the fashionable colour. I have seen her portraît, taken then, and she must have been lovely, though she did wear the stand-up collar—the *collet-monté*—of the time of Louis XIV. to please her mamma, who was somewhat old-fashioned in her tastes, and was

full of recollections of the brilliant entertainments she had seen at Marli.

"And Renée de l'Isle idolized her; but though
wealthy and noble—for in those days people
made a great fuss about their heraldry; to marry
was to get a coat of arms, quartered, impaled, or
so forth; now we are thankful if we marry a
good monogram.   So the world wags—*très bon!*
Well, though wealthy and noble, he was too
young to think of marriage, and so was Henriette.   A little time, and they should be happy,
for they were betrothed solemnly in the church
of Saint Pierre; but that little time was to be
spent by Renée in the army; and one morning
which brought him but a dubious throb of excitement and which filled Henriette's heart with
anguish, he found himself appointed a sub-lieu-
tenant in the Regiment of Mazarin (the 54th of
the old French Line, under the monarchy), as a
letter from the Minister of War, Lieutenant-
General the Duc de Choiseul, informed him.   So
now Damon and Pythias were to be separated.
The days of their joy were to terminate.

"The lovers were impulsive and young; so their
hearts were wrung with sorrow at parting.   Henriette gave Renée a white scarf embroidered by
her own hands with blue *nonpareille,* a narrow
ribbon then much used by ladies in decorating
silk or velvet, and weeping as if her heart would
break, she placed it round him, and then sank
into the arms of her mother.

" 'Oh, Henriette, cease to weep thus. Your life was never made for sorrow,' murmured Renée, as he hung over her pale face. 'It should be all love, kisses, and sunshine; and such shall it be, my beloved, when in two years I return.'

" '*Ah, mon Dieu!* two years!' she exclaimed, and would not be comforted; for two years seemed a long, long time indeed to look forward to.

" While Renée for a time could feel no military ardour, even while contemplating himself by the aid of his mother's great crystal-framed mirror in the white uniform, the scarlet vest, and gold-bound hat of the Regiment of Mazarin, he strove to comfort himself by remembering that in the scene before him the term of probation would soon glide away.

" But he could think only of Henriette, her tears and her fair beauty, her love and her promises of fidelity, and while posting away to the frontier of Germany, he longed to be again as he had been, a happy boy in the woods of Languedoc, conning over with Henriette the charming story, " La Belle au Bois dormant," and others, before they learned to relish the writings of Scuderi, Mademoiselle de la Fayette, and the Countess d'Auneuil. So they parted, but looked forward to the coming time when they could marry, and be happy for all the days of their lives, as the old stories have it.

" The following month the tears of Henriette

flowed afresh, for her only brother, Louis De la Fosse, was appointed to the Regiment of Languedoc, which was the 53rd of the old Line, prior to the Revolution of 1792; but though the numbers of their respective corps were so *near*, the friends were placed far apart; for while Renée was doing duty on the banks of the Rhine, Louis was sent to broil in Martinique for two years.

"In all that time he never heard of Renée, and but seldom of his own family. In those days there were no steamers, no telegraphic wires or deep sea cables; and the letters of those who were separated became indeed as the visits of angels, few and far between.

"However, the famous Treaty of Paris, by which France lost Canada and Louisiana, enabled her to bring home great numbers of her troops from far and foreign shores; thus the year 1764 saw the Regiment of Languedoc quartered in its native province; and as it marched into Montpellier to take quarters in the strong citadel which Louis XIV. had built, how great was the joy of Louis De la Fosse to find the Regiment of Mazarin drawn up to receive and salute it with all the honours of war, bayonets fixed and colours flying; for by a singular coincidence, the 54th had come in but a few days before from the Rhine.

"Mademoiselle De la Fosse had been taken to Paris by her parents, as her health had been delicate ; but the two young lieutenants speedily met and renewed their friendship amid the same scenes where it had first grown and been cemented, and for some days they were incessantly together before they remembered that they now unfortunately belonged to two regiments which had long been rivals in camp, field, and garrison; and following up some absurd feud, old, perhaps, as the latter days of the Cardinal, from whom the 54th was named, had fostered an unremitting hatred, which was apt to break out between the officers and men of each on the most trivial occasions. Such feuds were but too common then in the French service, and officers of hostile corps would fight, whenever they met, upon the least imaginary affront, even a glance, though when out of uniform they were the best friends in the world.

" The 53rd had been raised in Languedoc in 1672, and the Comte de Douglas was its Colonel at the time of our story. The 54th had been raised the year after, and was commanded by the Marshal Duc de Mazarin.*

" The friends knew of this spirit of folly, but it was nothing to them; they would soon be brothers, they loved each other dearly, and would never do otherwise. One evening they had dined together at the *Fleur d'Amour,* a cabaret in the

---

* " Liste Historique des Troupes de France."

Place du Peyron, a promenade outside the city, and as they sat at the open windows, which from the lofty terrace enabled them to survey all the old familiar views, their hearts swelled with happiness, and they grasped each other's hands.

"' Peste !' exclaimed Renée, 'but this is pleasanter work than lying on out picket before Frankfort !'

"' True, Renée, mon ami,' responded Louis. 'When looking down as we do on dear old Montpellier, with all its quaint, old-fashioned streets, and the groves and vineyards of our beautiful Languedoc, spreading yonder far away even to the Pyrenees, the blue Mediterranean in the distance, dotted with white sails, it seems as if it were but yesterday that we trudged together to college, with Livy, Horace, Juvenal, and Euclid in our satchels, and yet thousands of miles of ocean have rolled between us since then, and I have been among the Caribbean Isles, have seen the green savannahs of Martinique, and the lightning of a tropical tempest play round the summit of Mont Pelee !'

"' Morbleu ! but yesterday indeed, and yet an age since we saw Henriette—our Henriette, Louis !'

"' Let us be happy in the hope of seeing her soon ; and meantime, let us have a little turn at picquet, for here comes Gustave Lapierre of ours, a horrid quarrelsome fellow, with whom we had better have nothing to do.'

" So they seated themselves to picquet just as Lapierre, a tall, thin, and swaggering looking officer, with his triangular cocked hat very much over one eye, his left hand planted on the hilt of his sword, the fingers of his right twirling his moustache, entered the room, bowed to De la Fosse, gave a supercilious glance at the face of Renée and the uniform of the 54th, and with a loud and imperious voice, ordered wine and the ' Gazette Française.'

" Renée felt his face flush, but he affected to attend to his game, and he and his friend played for small sums, as neither of them ever gambled; but Renée, being annoyed by the presence and general bearing of Lapierre, played ill, and the run of the cards went in favour of Louis, who won every game.

" ' Pardonnez moi, Louis,' said Renée, laughing; ' but how is it possible that you always win so?'

" ' In what way?'

" ' Contriving *always* to have such excellent hands.'

" ' No contrivance at all, my dear Renée; 'tis chance; but keep your temper.'

" ' Could I lose it with you, Louis, when your voice and eyes so remind me of Henriette?'

" ' Well, cease to think so much of her, and the next game perhaps may be in your favour,' said Louis, laughing.

"'Hélas non!' sighed Renée, and again Louis laughed, for he won, and then they separated with an arrangement to meet on the morrow. De l'Isle repaired to his quarters in the citadel, while De la Fosse took his horse and rode off to his father's chateau, which stands on the road to Nismes, and is still a fine old place, though it was sorely battered and burned by the Hugue- nots in 1622.

"Lapierre had been an attentive listener to all that had passed; the imprudent jest of Renée at losing so often, the jocular hint at unfair play, and Louis's laughing advice that he should 'keep his temper.' Repairing straight to the citadel, he gathered a few of the quarrelsome spirits of the 53rd about him, and to them he retailed the story, but in such a manner that the whole af- fair took the tone of an affront passed upon the corps, through the regimental antagonism of the 54th, and he was deputed to represent to De la Fosse that he must 'demand immediate satis- faction alike for the sake of his own honour and that of the Regiment of Languedoc.'

"Louis was inexpressibly shocked when he heard how the matter was likely to turn, and felt inclined to pass his sword through the body of the meddlesome regimental bully who so smi- lingly confronted him; but that would not have mended the affair, though it might have bene- fited society, as Lapierre was a professional duellist, and had killed and wounded many men, by a peculiar feint followed by a thrust, of which he alone was master.

"'Come, come, comrade, you must have him out and kill him, or we shall be obliged to call out every officer of his corps in succession, and give them their *sauce Robert* to perfection.'

"Louis knew that this was meant by Lapierre as a sneer at the family of Renée, who was descended from Taillevant, Master of the Kitchen to Charles VII. of France, for whom he invented no less than seventeen different sauces; so the remark, which might have made him laugh at another time, inflamed him with passion at the speaker.

"'Beware, Gustave Lapierre,' said he, 'for if I am taunted to fight my dearest friend—which cannot be thought of—I shall fight with *you* next.'

"'Perhaps that cannot be thought of *either*,' sneered the other, with a contemptuous glance of his grey-green eyes, which were totally destitute of lashes; 'but as you please; I shall lay before the corps your doubts and scruples in this matter, and we shall solve them for you, *après la mode Française.*'

"'Dare you, Monsieur, impugn my courage?'

"'It seems I must; but the omission of that in your composition is a little oversight on the part of Providence for which you are in no way to blame,' sneered the other.

" 'Sangdieu, but I will kill you, Lapierre!'

" 'You may try; but you must first kill this Renée Taillevant De l'Isle.'

" Knowing but too well where all this tended, and aware of the fashion of the time, Louis at once sought out his friend, in a state of mind most difficult to describe.

" Duelling, I have said, was then alike a passion and a vice in French society; so it was carried to a pitch of ferocious madness in the army. Louis XV., and the two Louises his predecessors, had issued many an edict in vain against it, but the rage for fighting, wounding, and killing by the sword continued, though not quite so bad as in the time of Henri IV., during whose reign, as Lomenie records, no less than four thousand French gentlemen perished in single combat; and by the civil law of France, as it existed in 1764, the period referred to, ' the body of a person slain in a duel was ordained to be dragged through the streets on a sledge, and refused Christian burial;' but there were ways and means for evading this ordinance, as we shall see in the end.

" With sorrow and horror in their hearts, and with tears in their eyes, they found themselves compelled to take their swords and repair to a solitary part of the old rampart that girds Montpellier, and there, in presence of Gustave Lapierre and several officers of both regiments, they threw off their white uniforms, and engaged in their shirt sleeves, each as he did so seeking only to be wounded, rather than to wound, and to avoid meeting the glance of the other.

"'Guard, Louis—oh, mon Dieu—guard!' exclaimed De l'Isle.

"'Guard you, Renée; cover yourself well,' replied De la Fosse.

"'Enough of compliments—enough of griefs,' said Lapierre, scornfully; 'fall on, like French *gentlemen!*'

"'Would it were with thee!' exclaimed both together.

"'I am at your service, Messieurs, this affair once over.'

"In the peculiar manner they fought, they each received a sufficient number of flesh wounds with the sword's point to have satisfied even the artificial scruples of the spectators, and actually to disable themselves from continuing the conflict longer, for that day at least. So they separated and retired each to his quarters.

"The moment that Renée had his wounds dressed he presented himself before the senior officers of his regiment; but they one and all turned their backs upon him, with the taunt that he 'had been *forced* to fight.'

"'In the name of God and St. Denis, what more must we do?' asked Renée, in utter bewilderment.

" ' Fight till one is killed on the spot, or be
for ever disgraced among us as a couple of
poltroons !'

" ' He and you, and all of you who would say
so are liars and pitiful *capitaines !*' cried Renée,
transported with rage ; but their insulting laughter rang in his ears as he quitted the citadel, and
again sought the presence of his friend.

" In the distraction of their minds, they resolved that they should meet again on the morrow, rush simultaneously upon each other's swords
and die together !

" Early next morning, Louis De la Fosse was
seated in the library of the chateau, writing a
farewell letter to his parents and to Henriette,
when the latter suddenly appeared by his side.
Accompanied by her old nurse, she had preceded
their father and mother, who had loitered in
Montpellier ; but she had heard that with which
the whole city was ringing, that her affianced
husband had insulted her brother ; that they
had fought, and were to fight again.

" Fear was in her face, but in her eyes were
mingling a gleam of anger with the light of love,
for she idolized her brother. Her eyes were
beautifully set, with a half droop in the lids that
gave them great sweetness and softness, though
her short upper lip and chiselled nostrils—it is a
great word " chiselled," and I don't know how
we should ever get on without it—told of spirit
and will and high breeding too.

"'Oh, Louis! after our separation, what a meeting is this for us all!' she exclaimed, piteously.

"'Then you have heard all, my sister?'

"'Yes; that you have quarrelled, have fought, and hate each other so that though covered with bloody bandages, you are to fight again. Oh, Louis, my brother! tell me in pity can such things be?'

"'You have but come in time, sister, to see me before I die; for Renée and I have sworn, hand in hand, not to survive each other.'

"'Oh, this is a madness!'

"'It is the crime of others, Henriette.'

"Then he told her how they were situated; how the supposed quarrel and the duel had been forced upon them by the insane suggestion of a barbarous code of honour; and a great horror came over the heart of the girl, for she knew that the matter was irremediable, and she clung to his breast and wept in a paroxysm of grief and despair; till at last the fatal hour approached when he had to tear himself away, and leave her.

"'Farewell, Henriette, my sister, my sweet pet-bird! It is dreadful indeed to die so soon, and by dear Renée's hand too; but you shall see us again, and pray over us, when all is ended.'

"Alas! though she could not foresee it, even that melancholy office was denied her.

"To be brief, they met again upon the ramparts, when all the officers of both regiments were present, those of each corps eyeing the others with hostility, malevolence and exultation. The morning was cold and grey, not a bit of blue was visible in the sky; the sun, as he rose from the waters of the Mediterranean, was shrouded in dun and sombre coloured haze, and the wind came in fitful gusts and sighed mournfully through the embrasures of the old rampart. The two friends were deadly pale, their eyes were bloodshot, their handsome and usually cheerful faces wore an expression of intense sadness, for each felt himself forced into the commission of a dreadful crime, against which all his nature revolted. They moved with difficulty too, for their limbs were stiffened by the wounds of yesterday.

"The words to 'guard' and 'engage' were given by Lapierre, and with half-closed eyes they rushed upon each other's swords, and both fell at the same instant, each pierced by a dreadful wound.

"A cry of mingled agony and anguish escaped Renée; but from the quivering lips of Louis De la Fosse there came not a sound. He was pierced through the heart!

"While writhing himself forward to embrace his dead friend, Renée, whose wound was perilously near the left lung, was lifted up and borne away by some officers of the 54th to the house of a surgeon, where he was kept in concealment for three months, till his wound was cured so far

that he could fly and escape the civil authorities.
But to prevent the latter from putting in execution the final disgrace of the law upon the dead
body of Louis De la Fosse, the officers of the
53rd threw it into a hole which they had ready
dug for the purpose; and round that hideous
grave they stood in a ring, with their swords
drawn, till the remains were almost utterly con-
sumed by quicklime, so that the sentence I have
quoted elsewhere could not by any possibility be
put in force upon them; but prior to their destruction thus, Lapierre drew from his victim's
finger the onyx ring to which I have referred.
My father wore it for his lifetime and then
transmitted it to me.

"Renée De l'Isle fled from Montpellier in the
night, and perished of want in Spain; and so
ended this most barbarous tragedy!"

* * * * *

"And Mademoiselle De la Fosse; what became
of her?" asked Cyril, whom the little love bit of
the story interested.

"More like a heroine of romance than of real
life, she never married; but on proving her
eight quarters of nobility became a *Chanoinesse* in
the chapter of Ste. Marie, and lived to be a very
old, and, notwithstanding her brilliant beauty in
youth, a very ugly woman. Often have I sat
upon her knee in my infancy, for I was a great
pet of hers, and she loved me most perhaps for

bearing the name of Louis. She died so lately as 1818, when Louis XVIII. was king of France."

By the time the story of Colonel De la Fosse was ended, the shrill trumpets of the Zouaves and the brass drums of the French Infantry had been giving warning that the time was at hand when, without reference to rank, all should be in camp or quarters; so the *Restaurant de l'Armée d'Orient* began to empty fast, as each visitor departed to the *place d'armes* or head-quarters of his regiment. As that of De la Fosse (the 34th) lay encamped on the side of Varna nearest to the British lines, Cyril, Horace and he rode off together leisurely, just as the soft and very brief twilight began to close over the flat shore, the most unpicturesque city, with its four flat leaden domes, and the sea of white tents that spread over the plain to the westward of it.

" By Jove !" exclaimed Horace, " there is our captain of Zouaves again !"

" Where ?" asked De la Fosse, sharply, as he reined up his horse.

" Coming from among the tents of Omar Pasha's people."

" And he is *not* riding towards the lake of Devna, where the 1st Zouaves are under canvas, but quite in an opposite direction."

" At a devil of a pace too," added Cyril.

" Let us follow him. There is something in all this I don't like," said the French colonel.

Skirting the camp, and riding under the concealment of a long grove of olives, they followed him at a short distance, as they thought unseen; but on clearing the group of trees they could perceive that he had urged his little Tartar horse almost to racing speed, and was riding fast towards the sea.

As the brief twilight passed away, and darkness closed over the flat landscape, they lost all trace, but still rode on in the hope of overtaking, or perhaps meeting him when returning; and after continuing this vague pursuit for some miles, they found themselves on a lonely part of the sea coast some seven or eight miles from Varna, and near the port of Baldjik, where no sound broke the silence but the dash of the waves as they rolled on the shingle.

"Well, Messieurs," said Colonel De la Fosse, "we have had a bootless gallop."

"But see—there is some signal!" exclaimed Cyril.

About a mile from them, in the very direction they had come from, a small blue light was suddenly burned for a second or two, but close to the shore; another light upon the water responded, and then came the half-muffled sound of oars in the rowlocks distinctly over the surface of the sea. Then all became still but the dull clang of their horses' hoofs, as the trio galloped along the sands to where the mysterious lights had shone.

Alone on the shore, with ears drooping, stood

the little Tartar horse, minus saddle, bridle, and
holsters; a scarlet Zouave turban and blue
Zouave jacket lay near; and about two miles at
sea, but visible nevertheless, was a large lugger
or small schooner—which you will—with all her
canvas spread, standing away to the north-east out
of the Gulf of Baba, as if heading for that portion
of the Black Sea which runs towards the Isthmus
of Perecop, in the rear of Sebastopol, before which
the British fleet lay.

"Death and the devil!" exclaimed the French
colonel, "we have had a spy among us; but the
fellow, however daring, overacted his part of
Frenchman. Ah, *morbleu!* there will be no need
for me to visit the camp of the 1st to-morrow;
our friend, 'the Zouave captain,' is in yonder
craft, with all the information he has been able
to glean up in and about Varna, and a few hours
hence will lay it all before Prince Mentschicoff."

They were intensely annoyed to find that he
had escaped them;* but regrets were useless

---

* The episode of a Russian spy at Varna was not without
a parallel during the siege. "A captain of Zouaves was ob-
served in the French trenches for the last four or five days.
As he was always bothering the men working at their guns,
the officer commanding the battery called out, 'Who is that
captain of Zouaves that is interfering with my men, and not
attending to his duty.' The fellow appeared confused, and
the men began 'to smell a rat.' He jumped over the
works, and though fired upon, got safely into Sebastopol."

now. Wedderburn and Ramornie returned to their camp in the Vale of Aladyn, bidding farewell to De la Fosse *en route;* but the information he had given in the restaurant proved to be quite correct; for the 5th of September saw the long lines of tents struck on the plain—the charnel-house—of Varna, the great armament embarked for the Crimea, and the smoke of the steamers alone visible from the ramparts when the sun set on the shores of the Black Sea.

CHAPTER III.

WE have small space for much detail of the Crimean War, and so shall confine ourselves chiefly to the personal adventures of our *dramatis personæ* there. But it seems strange to think how after the lapse of a very few years the terrors, the tears, the sufferings, and the glory incident to that campaign, are already half forgotten, and the whole seems but as a tale that is told ! Yet great were the endurance, steady the discipline, and noble the heroism of those who followed Raglan, our one-armed veteran, to the field ; and there were men of all ages in his army, from those white-haired warriors who like himself had seen the night of horrors at Badajoz, and the corpse-strewn plains of Vittoria and Waterloo, down to the fair-cheeked boy-ensigns fresh from school ; for when the death-lists of the Crimea appeared, many a name therein was recalled with pride and sorrow in the class-rooms and playgrounds of Eton, Harrow, and Rugby.

Yes, it is indeed all as a tale that is told—-the

night of our landing at Eupatoria, when without
tents or baggage sixty thousand men remained
on the bare ground, under torrents of rain, thus
adding fearfully to the scourge of cholera next
day; the march towards the enemy under a
blazing sun; the maddening thirst, that thousands broke their ranks and rushed to quench in
the Bulganac; the skirmish there with our advanced guard; the heights of the Alma bristling
with cannon and bayonets; the death ride of " the
Six Hundred" at Balaclava, when cannon blazed
in front, on flank, and in *rear* of them; that
dull November morning, when amid the grey
mists the rumble of the Russian artillery was
heard while Mentschicoff poured his hordes into
the valley of Inkerman, and the butchery of our
wounded there and in the quarries. Then came
the half-frozen trenches and rifle pits, while the
iron voice on the grassy slopes of the Mamelon,
the lines of the Redan, and the mighty batteries
of Sebastopol was never still; and though last,
not least, the ghastly horrors of the great hospital
at Scutari !

On the morning of the 20th September, the
allied army was face to face with the Russians,
led by Prince Alexander Mentschicoff, and then
intrenched on the heights above the Alma, a
stream which rises among the western slopes of
Crim-Tartary, and falls into the sea twelve miles
from Sebastopol.

Cyril Wedderburn had been on active service before in India, but this was to be Horace's first battle; and such was also the case with most of the young subalterns in the army.

High on the southern bank of the Alma rises a ridge of picturesque rocks, which terminate in a cliff which overhangs the Euxine; in the ravines of these rocks grew groves of turpentine and other trees, many of which had been felled to form *abattis* to encumber the advance of our troops. The Russian lines were formed along that ridge, two miles in length, and by the aid of field-glasses their flat caps, their spiked helmets, glittering bayonets, and grey-coated masses, could be seen as the allied columns came on. Every available point was mounted with cannon, trenches were dug, redoubts and breastworks thrown up, and on the Kourganè Hill, six hundred feet above the Alma, to protect his right, Mentschicoff had constructed an enormous triangular battery, mounted with heavy cannon and 24-pounder howitzers. There too was the great Kazan column with the holy image of St. Sergius, and also, oddly enough, a train of carriages full of ladies from Sebastopol and Bagtche Serai, "the Seraglio of Gardens," waiting to see the defeat of the "Island curs," as they termed the British, whom, strangely enough, they believed to be chiefly seamen.

The morning of the Alma was a lovely one.

From the Black Sea, where our steamers—their smoke ascending high into the clear air—were creeping in shore to shell the Russian left, there came a soft breeze that played along the slopes, and whirled in wreaths the smoke from the blazing Tartar village of Burliuk. The leaves rustled pleasantly in the beautiful groves of olive and turpentine trees, and a peculiar fragrance that filled the air came from the leaves of a little aromatic herb (which grew there wild) when bruised by the feet of the marching column, or the wheels of the field artillery. Many places were covered with orange-coloured crocuses, growing thick as buttercups, in the fields at home.

"It was now that after forty years of peace the great nations of Europe were once more meeting for battle!"

The enemy was at last in front—those dark grey masses, so often spoken of, written of, and thought of—the hordes of half-savage Russia, and as the Fusileers (under Sir Edward Elton, who was mounted on his black barb Vidette, and looked every inch an English soldier) with the rest of their division halted, the altered demeanour of the officers and men became apparent to themselves. All foolish banter and idle conversation had ceased. There was indeed a cessation of sound—a kind of hush—over all the army, save when the neigh of a horse, or the clatter of a field-gun, woke the echoes of the rocks in front.

No man, unless a fool, goes into action, especially for the first time, in the same mood of mind with which he enters a ball-room, or joins a dinner party. Decent gravity pervaded the entire ranks, and many a heart was doubtless filled with prayer and thoughts of home and loved ones far away. Now and then a brotherly emotion of anxiety for Cyril occurred to Horace Ramornie, and to Cyril for him. Which might survive the day to speak of the other? If both fell, would they be buried together?

"Bother such thoughts!" muttered Horace, as he ventured to light a cigar in rear of his company.

They and others waxed a little more kind in their bearing to those about them; and one or two who had small coolnesses, shook hands or bowed and smiled in passing. Some, like Joyce the married captain, leant thoughtfully on their swords; and he, poor fellow, was thinking, no doubt, of the two little faces he had last seen, side by side and asleep in the dingy room at Chatham Barracks on the morning of the march.

Sir Edward sat motionless on his horse, till an aide-de-camp, passing at a quick trot—he was Nolan—the gallant and heroic Nolan—said—

"The General wishes the men to get loose their cartridges. This, Sir Edward, will be a field day for most of us to remember."

Elton repeated the order; and under their bearskin caps a grim kind of smile lit up the faces of the Fusileers, as they opened their pouches and loosened the ammunition from its packing paper.

In losing Mary Lennox, life had—for a time at least—lost much of its charm for Cyril Wedderburn; and somehow on this morning he felt as if danger and death had been for him divested of half their terrors; and he had the longing desire to do that which rarely falls to the lot of those of subaltern rank, something great and brilliant; something that would make his family and friends —aye, even the lost Mary—proud of him; yet with all this wild enthusiasm he seemed perfectly cool and unmoved.

But alas for poor Cyril! as we shall see in the sequel, he longed and hoped in vain for such distinction as he honestly coveted! And he looked wistfully at the armed and hostile heights with the thought that it would be hard to die there without leaving his mark upon the world —some footprint " on the sands of Time."

" Breathless and exhausting work this is, gentlemen," said Sir Edward Elton, taking off his bearskin to cool his forehead, for the heat was intense, and the troops had been some hours under it.

" It suggests vague desires of iced champagne," said Jack Probyn.

" Egad, it's mighty glad I'd be of a glass of pale ale, and a pipeful of birdseye or cavendish," added Beamish; " but here comes a Frenchman who has been on some final mission I hope to Lord Raglan."

" Colonel De la Fosse, by Jove !" exclaimed Horace, as that officer trotted past the British lines. " Good morning, Colonel—are we likely to come to blows soon ?"

" Soon enough, it may be, for the Russians yonder, Monsieur," replied De la Fosse, pausing. " The moment I rejoin Bosquet the attack will commence. I have been pretty close to those Russian fellows already. They look resolute and determined ; but what of that? We shall teach them that to win glory or die in the field, is all a soldier need care for."

" Well," said old Major Singleton, " I should prefer half-pay with a snug pension myself."

" Every man to his taste, mon camarade," replied the Frenchman gaily, as he laughed and galloped off to the right, of which the French had contrived to possess themselves, and an awkward post of honour they might have found it, close by the sheer cliffs which overhung the Euxine, had they been defeated, or had the British left been turned.

After two protracted halts, during one of which the French division of Bosquet, coolly cooked their coffee and made a comfortable breakfast ;

and after two consultations between Lord Raglan
and Marshal St. Arnaud (who had taken the field
in almost a dying condition), and after the troops
had been irritated by seeing parties of Cossacks
scouring the ground in front, while the flash of
steel could be seen amid the olive groves and
breastworks above the Alma, and at times a
Russian standard brandished as if in defiance of
the lines that were approaching, now wheeling,
now deploying, extending and taking ground to
the right or left—a roar of musketry far away
on the right flank announced that the fiery
French had begun the attack, and were pouring forward in impetuous masses under a terrible shower
of missiles of every kind. These masses were
chiefly the fierce and active little Zouaves, flushed
with their victories in Africa, and they were seen
to swarm up the heights at the point of the
bayonet, in their blue jackets and baggy red
breeches, till they formed in two lines, and with
a truly French yell, rushed on to close with the
enemy !

On went our columns to close with them too,
opening fire at half-past one. By that time, the
cannon shots fell thick and fast among our ranks.
Bursting at times in mid air, the shrill whistling
shells fell in iron showers among them; others
ripped up the earth, scattering stones and splinters
on every side. Now a bullet swept past unseen
with a deep humming sound; the next might

tear a man in two, or hurl him away, doubled up like a muslin scarf; another would bury itself deep in the ranks, making a lane of blood and death, of shrieks and agony.

"The slow ping, ping, *ping* of those Minié rifles—don't at all like it," said Probyn.

"Daresay not," replied little Meredyth Pomfret, whose face was flushed with boyish ardour and pride in carrying the Queen's colours. "But why particularly so?"

"It is such deliberate potting, always suggesting that every bullet takes a human life."

"Well, it is just what a soldier's work is," replied the boy, bravely. "By jingo; let us only get close to them!"

The burning village with its flaming stack-yards formed the centre of the British position.

To the right of it the 41st Welsh and 49th regiments forded the Alma under a heavy fire from Minié rifles of the Russians who there lay snugly *perdue* in rear of some vineyard walls, over which the purple grapes were hanging in ripe and heavy clusters; while on the left of Burliuk the whole Light Division under old Sir George Brown (who had first smelt powder at the capture of Copenhagen in 1807) dashed across the stream and proceeded to storm the heights, which were so steep in some places, that in several instances the enemy's bullets traversed the

spinal column, as they were shot sheer down upon
the assailants.

Cyril's regiment was in the same division with
the 33rd, the Welsh Fusileers, the 19th, 77th, and
88th, all which pressed on with such fury that
they speedily routed the Russian riflemen out of
the vineyards, carrying the walls at the point of
the bayonet, and pushing on beyond these, a few
only pausing at times to snatch a handful of
those grapes which proved so delicious to men
furiously excited, and sorely athirst, after their
long march in a hot and breathless morning.

Waving their caps and swords in front, their
officers led them on, amid tumultuous cheers.

" Forward, the Fusileers !"

"·Forward, Twenty-third !"

" On, on—Nineteenth and Seventy-seventh !"

" Forward, forward ! aim under the cross-
belts."

Such were the cries from officers and men on
all hands, as the scarlet tide pressed upward;
but they were mingled with many a shriek and
groan, for the Russian shot fell thick as hail,
and every moment the dead and wounded were
dropping in the ranks. But now began that
famous up-hill charge, by which the field was
won; the dark Rifles meanwhile taking the hills
in flank, as coolly as if at drill on Chatham Lines.

The supports were the Duke of Cambridge's
Division of Guards and Highlanders.

Cyril could see before him but a cloud of smoke, amid which, at times half seen, half lost, were the figures of Sir George Brown, on a grey charger, and Sir Edward Elton, on his black one. A shower of lead, heavier than usual, tore through the ranks of the division. Colonel Chesters, of the Twenty-third, and eight of his officers, fell almost at the same moment, and their brave Welshmen were nearly decimated. Sir George Brown fell amid a cloud of dust, and, for a moment, it was supposed that he was killed.

The Royal Fusileers then wavered for a moment, but reformed, shoulder to shoulder, as Sir George sprang to his feet and again led on the whole. The first of Sir Edward's officers who fell was Captain Joyce; a bullet shattered his head and his body rolled down hill. The three next were Bingham, Jack Probyn, and young Pomfret. The first was literally cut in two by a round shot; the second was pierced in the heart by a ball, and bounded into the air ere he fell dead. The third had the standard-pole splintered in his hand by a ball, which penetrated his breast, and he was left behind to die in great agony. Ned Elton snatched the colours from his relaxed hand; but in a minute after he too fell, a leg being smashed by a Minié bullet. Relief after relief were shot under that fatal colour; but still the human tide went rolling upward and onward, cheering wildly as their growing enthusiasm became mingled with a thirst for vengeance, and a longing to grapple with the foe!

A roar, as of thunder, was in the air, and a hell of fire seemed in front of them.

Meanwhile, wounded officers and men, in hundreds, were being borne to the rear by bandsmen, on stretchers, or crawling to the river side to quench their thirst—in many instances the thirst of the dying. Though nine hundred of all ranks fell on the slope of the great redoubt, amid the vineyards and the perilous abattis of trees; and though the colours of the Twenty-third Welsh Fusileers were actually planted on it, and the Russians expelled by the bayonet, the victory was not yet decided.

From a higher range of the hills, there rushed upon our now breathless, blown, and shattered troops, a heavy double column of Russian Infantry—the regiments of Onglitz and Vladimir; one wearing flat caps, the other with spike-helmets. A great, grey, solid mass, they come on with equal ardour and fury, strong in the belief of the conquest which the Bishop of Moscow had predicted would accompany the image they bore—that of St. Sergius—a hideous idol of carved and painted wood.

It was then that the British ranks began to waver, and even to fall back a little way, leaving in and near the redoubt several wounded, who

were mercilessly bayonetted, or brained by the
clubbed muskets of the advancing Russians, who,
in some instances, hewed off fingers in their
eagerness to possess the rings of those they
murdered.

By this time, no less than nineteen serjeants
of the Thirty-third had perished, chiefly in defence
of the regimental colours ; and most fatal would
the temporary repulse have been, but for the re-
advance of that corps, with the Fusileers and the
Guards and Highlanders of the Duke's division,
when the conflict was renewed in all its fury.

The appearance of the Highlanders, in their
strange costume, as their brigade advanced in
successive *échelon* of regiments, with their tartans
and black plumes waving in the wind, seemed to
impart some superstitious terror to the Russians,
who almost immediately began to waver.

A close and deadly volley was poured upon
them. No sound in particular followed, save the
yells of the wounded, while the Highlanders
" cast about" to reload ; but after their next
volley, a strange rattling was heard, as the
bullets fell fast among the tin canteens and
kettles which the enemy carried outside their
knapsacks, for they were all *right-about-face* now.
Then a cry—a literal wail of despair—came from
them, as they broke their ranks and fled, throwing away muskets, packs, caps, and everything
that might impede their speed.

Holy Russia was no longer invincible ! " The

Angel of Light had departed from her, and the Demon of Death had come!" Three generals, seven hundred prisoners, and about seven hundred and fifty of their wounded, remained in our hands, according to Mr. Kinglake, though other authorities have given them as many, many more.

The Heights of the Alma were won; but three thousand three hundred of the Allies lay killed and wounded on their green slopes, which were dotted for miles by spots in scarlet, blue, or grey—each *spot* a human corpse, or a man in mortal agony from bayonet or gun-shot wounds!

Among the latter was Cyril Wedderburn!

At the very moment when his splendid, but sorely cut-up regiment, led by Sir Edward Elton, was rushing with the bayonet in pursuit of the foe beyond the Kourganè Hill, he was lying near the river, covered with blood and dust, and presenting a piteous spectacle. On two crossed muskets he had been borne there, to have his maddening thirst quenched and his wounds attended to.

When the troops were recoiling, after the capture of the great redoubt, he had found himself close to Horace Ramornie, who was endeavouring to assist a Russian officer of rank, as the number of his medals and stars evinced, and who was lying, half smothered, under his dying horse, in the chest of which a cannot-shot was imbedded.

They succeeded in dragging him out, and raised him to his feet; but the barbarian—in whom, with the speed of thought, Cyril recognised the spy of Varna, the pretended Captain of Zouaves—drew a revolver from his belt, and, inspired by all the terror of capture, and the hatred of race and religion—for by these emotions his face, a handsome one, was quite distorted—he fired at both his protectors, and retired among his advancing men, escaping several shots that were sent after him by the exasperated Fusileers.

Horace escaped uninjured, but poor Cyril had his left arm wounded by one ball, while another penetrated his left breast. He sank into the arms of his kinsman, who uttered a cry of mingled rage and commiseration, and had him borne to the rear by two of the band; but he could do no more, having to lead his company, of which he was now the only surviving officer.

By this time, the Turks and French were in full pursuit of the enemy, whose last efforts were a few faint struggles, and a disorderly and scattered fire. Hereditary hatred and religious rancour alike inspired the Turks, whose shrill cries of " Allah, Allah Hu !" came, at times, upon the wind; for they still boast themselves to be the *Assakiri Mansurei Mohamediyes* — the " Victorious troops of Mohamed," and until the day of Balaclava they had always fought with honour.

CHAPTER IV.

IT was not until the next day that Horace could discover—and only after a long, painful, and exciting search—where his cousin Cyril was lying, and had lain all night, in extreme suffering and misery.

The night after the storming of the Russian intrenched camp, Horace slept soundly—the deep sleep of that utter exhaustion consequent to intense bodily toil, the heat of the march before the engagement, and over exhaustion of the mind. He did awake once or twice, to see around him, as in a confused dream, the darkness of the chilly night, and, that something of the picturesque might not be wanting, groups of soldiers, lying or sitting, and smoking or chatting round fires of turpentine, olive and willow trees, of Russian muskets and gun carriages, that flamed high above their heads, and caused the piles of muskets to glitter in light. These were the men who, but a few hours before, had been amid all that wild carnage, and were now quietly toasting little scraps of food in the blaze by which they warmed themselves, and which lit up their bronzed faces with a ruddy glow, and displayed their varied and, in many instances, torn and blood-stained uniforms.

Some were moaning over a wounded arm, or a bloody and recently bandaged stump, which they rested on a bed of branches, and thousands were lying about, in every attitude expressive of exhaustion.

So most of the army passed the night after we won the Alma; though some who were less worn out than others spent it in seeking over the field for those whom few or none could help them to find.

By the first ray of dawn, and while the red sun was rising above those hills that, on one side, look down on Simpheropol, and on the other overhang the windings of the fatal Alma, Horace, with a few of the Fusileers, had left the bivouac, and, without seeking food or refreshment, engaged in the melancholy and heart-rending task of searching over the field for his cousin, Cyril Wedderburn.

The two bandsmen by whom he had been borne away had been killed subsequently, and no one could say where they had laid him down, to bleed to death of his wounds, too probably.

Horace thought sadly of the many fine fellows gone for ever—those whose faces he should never look upon again; Jack Probyn, with whom he had played so many keen games at billiards; Bingham, whose handsome figure and winning manner made him a favourite with all women; Joyce, poor old Singleton (the man with the secret sorrow), and merry little Meredyth Pomfret, who was such a first-rate "bat," and so many of the brave rank and file too. He was full of depressing and harrowing thoughts.

Unstripped by "death-hunters," or a plundering peasantry (as those were who fell in the wars of Wellington, and left bare and ghastly under the eye of heaven), the soldiers here were all lying, whether dead or wounded, fully clothed and accoutred, just as the shot had struck them down in their ranks.

Many of the killed lay on their back, with their arms uplifted, as if still levelling their muskets, in all the cataleptic stiffness which so often results from gunshot wounds. "The upstretched arms of dead men were ghastly in the eyes of some; others thought they could envy the soldier released at last from his toil, and encountering no moment of interval between hard fighting and death." And over this scene rose the cloudless sun of a lovely September morning, glowing on the tender green of the willow and olive groves tossing their leaves in the warm, soft breeze, and suggestive of delicious tranquillity rather than the carnage of war.

The unfortunate braves of the Welsh Fusileers lay over each other literally in piles, amid dark pools of blood, in which the flies were battening; and wherever the cannon shot had bowled in their deadly career, lay bodies without legs, or heads, or arms, crushed, rent, and torn in some instances out of all semblance of humanity; and there were grey haired officers who had fought in other lands, in India, Persia, and Afghanistan, lying side by side with our poor boy-subalterns, slain in all the splendour of their *first* red coat—fresh from school and from their parents' arms.

Many a familiar face of his own corps was seen by Horace as he passed along, but they were pallid and still; no glance of recognition came back from the fixed and glazed eyes; no smile was on the open marble mouth. Among others, he saw young Meredyth Pomfret, lying dead with his hands as if yet clutching the colour-staff, the belt of which was still over his shoulder. He turned away with a sinking heart, and he knew that Cyril could not be there.

All who could speak were inquiring for water, or to learn when they would be taken to the rear and have their sufferings alleviated. Others begged only for a match or a pipeful of tobacco.

In their long grey coats, in many instances cuffed and collared with scarlet, the grim Russians lay thick, like swathes in a harvest field, along the Kourganè Hill, and all about the great

redoubt. Many had fallen in the act of reload-
ing, and lay with a steel ramrod in their hand,
or a half bitten cartridge between their teeth.
A ghastly grin or defiant smile was visible in
some of their dead faces; and in many instances
there were men of the 23rd and other corps of
the Light Division, who appeared to have perished
in the act of supplication or entreaty.

These were the wounded whom the merciless
Russians butchered, when the division wavered
on the crest of the hill.

Hairy knapsacks, glazed helmets, and the
coarse, clumsy firelocks of the Russian infantry
lay scattered there in thousands, just as they had
been cast away; and clouds of ammunition paper
were whirling over the sward.

Many acts of perfidy, similar to that by which
Cyril fell, had been perpetrated by the enemy.
In some instances our soldiers were shot down
by the wounded whom they were supplying with
water from their canteens. In this manner,
Captain Eddington of the 95th perished under
the eyes of his brother, who fell in the attempt
to avenge him; and enraged by such treacheries,
our soldiers clubbed their muskets and dashed
out the brains of the perpetrators, as creatures
totally unworthy of mercy or life.

Horace felt his heart growing more and more
sick as he looked around him, and heard the incessant and afflicting exclamations of suffering,

the result of wounds of every kind, and in all parts of the tender human form; stabs by bayonets, cuts by swords, musket shots, and the more dreadful casualties inflicted by cannon balls, grape, canister, and splintered shells; and if his tongue clove to the roof of his mouth with the intensity of his thirst, he thought, " What must these poor creatures be enduring!"   But ere long the regimental and naval surgeons, with fatigue parties and seamen from the fleet, began to be busy among them.

Wandering down from the heights by the extreme British right, he came among the wounded of the French left flank, and there the Zouaves were lying thick as leaves in autumn.   Two, who had each a limb bandaged tight by a bloody handkerchief, were seated with their backs against a large stone, smoking cigarettes, while a pretty vivandière, in a smart blue jacket and scarlet skirt, with the number of some regiment embroidered on her cap and shoulder-straps, was tripping about giving mouthfuls of brandy from her little barrel.

" Is she not charming—Pauline of ours!" exclaimed one of the smokers, admiringly.

" Mais certainement oui, charmante!" responded the other, and with great politeness they both saluted Horace as he passed them, though unable to rise; " and like ourselves she has breakfasted *à la carte* on grapes and cold water, most likely."

" Your regiment must have suffered severely," said he, " if we are to judge by the numbers lying here."

" Oui, Monsieur, we have lost twice as many as we did at Constantine. Diable! la fortune de la guerre est bien capricieuse!"

" True, Adrien," said the other, laughing; " but we gave those Muscovites a sharp taste of our little Charlemagnes—our cabbage-cutters;" for so the French soldiers name their sword-bayonets.

A man on the ground with his head propped upon some loose stones, attracted the eye of Horace at a little distance, for he was an officer and in the scarlet uniform of the Royal Fusileers, and proved to be Major Singleton !

He hastened to him, and found that he was just expiring of wounds, which a staff-surgeon, a somewhat elderly officer, had just been examining with great tenderness and care. The latter held up his hand warningly to Horace, as if to say, " Do not speak—it is useless." He had been pierced by two balls, each of which had inflicted a mortal wound. His filmy eye dilated as Horace bent over him; then his jaw fell, the breath passed away, and the brave soldier who, yesterday had been face to face with the Russians, was now face to face with—his Maker.

" We can but leave him till the burial party comes," said Dr. Riversdale, with great emotion;

for, by a singular fatality, it was in his hands, almost in his arms, that the first husband of Isabel Vane—poor Conyers Singleton, died! "Another officer of your corps," he added, "is lying near the river severely wounded—a Captain Wedderburn."

"In which direction?" asked Horace, starting.

"Where those turpentine bushes are. I have just dressed his wounds."

"Oh, how shall I thank you! It is he I have been in search of. Are the wounds dangerous?"

"One may prove so. A ball has entered the left breast, and injuring the lung, has passed out under the shoulder-blade. I am not without hopes of him, however."

Horace hurried in the direction indicated, and there amid the turpentine bushes, the branches of which were quite alive with brown larks and golden linnets, unscared by the din of yesterday, in full melody, lay him he sought!

Cyril was lying on his back and breathing heavily; his handsome face was pale as marble, and with his thick curly brown hair and well-curved moustache, Horace thought he looked like a manly and beautiful statue. His eyes were closed, but a quiver of agony at times passed over his features. His epaulettes had been torn off, probably by some passing Tartar of Burliuk. His uniform was open and sorely soiled, for bloody bandages traversed his breast. His whole aspect

was intensely pitiable and forlorn.   Alas for
Cyril! once so particular in his toilet, in the
quality of his perfumes, the exquisite fit of his
gloves and boots, and the general perfection of
his apparel.   His sword was still lying near his
hand, and on hearing a step, he instinctively
clutched it nervously, thus causing the blood to
well forth anew from the wound in his breast.

Poor Horace was deeply moved.

"Oh, Cyril," thought he, "if that poor mother
who dotes on you were to see you thus, sodden
and damp with dew, splashed with blood and
pierced with wounds!   Cyril!"

He opened his eyes, and a faint smile of recognition passed over his face as he took the hand
of his cousin, who knelt by his side.

"Thank Heaven you have escaped, Horace,"
said he.

"Yes, Cyril, my dear fellow.   Would to God
that you had been so fortunate.   I had my left
epaulette shot away by one bullet, my cap knocked
off by another, and my sword hand grazed by the
splinter of a shell, but I am untouched.   If that
Russian scoundrel—the spy——"

" He may have got his deserts by this time and
be lower than he has brought me.   You will
write to my father—say, to break all this gently
to my mother; but then she will unfortunately
see the Gazette first!" said Cyril, and now his
voice failed him.

After a time he asked—

" Who of ours have fallen, and who escaped ?"

" I know not who have escaped, but I know
that Bingham, Jack Probyn, Joyce, and Pomfret
are all gone.   Ned Elton had a leg smashed
under the colours, and poor Conyers Singleton
is lying dead among some stones yonder."

" Poor Joyce—his wife and children—he loved
them so !"

" The Colonel had his black horse shot under
him, and then led the regiment on foot."

" I feel utterly sick of life, Horace.   I hope
I shall die—and I must, if this agony endures,"
said Cyril in a low voice through his clenched
teeth.

" Do not speak or think thus.   You shall soon
be comfortably cared for.   The wounded are
ordered to be sent on board the fleet, and I shall
ee you off among the first."

Yesterday Cyril really had a mad desire to
court danger—to tempt death, but not to be
stricken down thus—almost assassinated, when
assisting in an act of mercy !   Yet why should he
have wished for death ? he began to think now.
Did not his tender mother, his affectionate and
manly father, love him, and Bob too, after his
somewhat cold and legal fashion ? All his brother
officers were his friends.   The passing emotion
was morbid and ungrateful ; yet, as he lay there,
he sighed in his soul for one glance from Mary's
eye—one touch of Mary's hand again !

Just as Horace was about to leave him in quest of assistance, a little midshipman with four seamen bearing stretchers passed near, and he hailed them. Into one of these he was carefully, even tenderly, lifted, and conveyed towards the shore, while Horace, with a prayer of hope that he might recover soon—for he and Cyril were especial friends—turned away to attend to his duties with the now shattered regiment—and these duties were the reverse of cheerful.

Many vessels sailed with their melancholy freights for Scutari; but on the voyage of three hundred and thirty miles which lie between that place and the mouth of the Alma, many a body was committed, coffinless, to the waves of the Euxine; for many brave fellows were uselessly shipped who were mortally wounded, and through routine, circumlocution, and infamous parsimony, "there were not medical necessaries on board for five out of fifty sufferers."*

"Ten men per company to bury the dead!" was the order issued to each regiment on the morning of the 21st September.

During the two days subsequent to the battle, Horace was so busy with one of the working parties who were ordered to separate the dead from the wounded; to bury the former and get the latter out of the field; collecting the abandoned Russian arms and destroying them by

---

* Letter of a medical officer.

fire, or otherwise, that he could barely snatch a
few minutes to dispatch a letter to Gwenny—
think what his aunt might of it, he could not
resist the temptation of writing to *her*—with a
brief detail of all that had transpired.

And from this pleasant office which brought
her bright face and sweet presence and all the
distinct *individuality* of the girl so vividly before
him, it was hard to turn to the grim task of
having those ghastly trenches dug, tenanted, and
filled up.

Though reflective, he was not much of a senti-
mentalist; yet as he stood by one of those heca-
tombs and heard the solemn words of the sur-
pliced regimental chaplain, reading the English
burial service—now that the fury of the battle
had passed away, his soul was stirred. "The
bitter pains of eternal death;" "The certain
hope of a resurrection to eternal life;" "For a
thousand years are in Thy sight as yesterday,
seeing that is past as a watch of the night. As
soon as Thou scatterest them, they are even as
a sleep, and fade away suddenly like the grass."

An old sergeant of the Welsh Fusileers, whose
son lay in that grave, all belted and accoutred
as when in life, made the responses tremulously,
and Horace felt moved by an emotion of great
pity.

To what end, or for what useful purpose, had
all this carnage been? Why had all those strong

and, many of them, handsome young men been cut off thus in the flower of their manhood ? For a time he thought war horrible—an utter desecration of God's fair earth ; but anon the trench was filled, the drums beat for dinner, and the living soon forgot those dead with whom they might be sleeping on the morrow.

"My poor fellows ! there lie one hundred and sixty of them !" said Sir Edward Elton, as he stood at the head of the long trench, with his sword-arm slung in his crimson sash ; " by this time they have learned the grand secret that lies between Time and Eternity. Well—well ! God rest them ! General and drum-boy, king and clown, we must all lie alike in our graves ; there is no distinction there !"

CHAPTER V.

WOUNDED AND MISSING.

THE summer was past, and the mellow tints of its successor were beginning to steal over the woods at Willowdean. September had come, the month of in-gathering, and brown autumn, the evening of the year, was creeping on.

There is usually then a great variety of tints in the Scottish woods; all gradations of green, from the tender paleness of the willow to the bronze-like branches of the sombre pine, mingling with every shade of fading foliage, from bright yellow to russet, brown, and red.

Autumn was beautiful as ever in the fertile Merse; the cattle lowed as usual on the pastoral hills of the Lammermuirs, over which the sun cast the flying shadows of the white clouds that came from the German Sea.

In the household at Willowdean, as elsewhere over all the British Isles, the public prints were eagerly scanned for their contents at that time; and the slow progress of our army in the East was watched with the keenest interest, for there were few in the land who had not either a relative or a friend who faced the pestilence at Varna, and the perils of war that followed it.

And every letter that came from the camp added to the craving for another; but during this anxious and eventful autumn, Willowdean House did not seem to wear its usual aspect. Lady Wedderburn had not her general circle of guests, and no friends were invited to pass the shooting season with Sir John. Robert was not much of a sportsman, so the gun-room was un-entered, the preserves remained undisturbed, and the speckled grouse and the golden pheasants kept holiday together, the latter venturing even to feed among the barnyard fowls at the home farm.

Robert Wedderburn was far from being insensible to the beauty of Gwenny, and still more to the pleasing fact that she was an heiress; and, regardless alike of his brother and cousin, he had striven to effect a footing in her good graces from the time Horace departed; but strove in vain : for Gwenny's impulsive and susceptible heart was far away with our army of the East. His futile attentions, however, had been apparent enough to Lady Wedderburn, and had secretly pleased her.

"If Gwenny should happen not to care for Cyril," thought she, "let Robert have her by all

means.   Her fortune would quite enable him to
cut the Temple and the dry study of the law."

Alone, the girl thought ever of the absent
Horace Ramornie; and all the scenes they had
been wont to visit, even the objects of nature,
seemed to the fanciful Gwenny full of his
memory by association of ideas.   The gurgle of
the clear trouting stream that came from the
hills and flowed under the old bridge in the
Dean, or *Den,* which being fringed by over-
arching willows, gave a name to the place; the
voices of the birds, the thrush, the blackbird and
woodlark, among the shrubberies of the garden
and the stately trees of the lawn, where they
always sang most joyously after a shower had
gemmed every leaf and flower; the sweet perfume of the clover fields, where many a day they
had ridden together and rushed their horses at
the fences and turf-dykes, all somehow reminded
Gwenny of Horace, the first and only love of
her passionate girlhood, now far away facing
peril and hardship, it might be to return no
more!

That a change had come over her, even when
visitors were present, was perceptible alike to
Sir John and to Lady Wedderburn.   The latter
flattered herself that she was at last thinking of
Cyril—that she had begun to see his merits, and
to remember how attractive he was in person
and manner; but the former more shrewdly

suspected the real state of matters, for Gwenny could not control her change of colour when the name of Horace was mentioned incidentally, though she betrayed no emotion whatever when that of his cousin occurred.

She never opened the piano now. To sing when Horace was no longer there to listen or to accompany her; to laugh and talk or seem to enjoy the society of others when he was absent—oh, what might he not be enduring!—proved a bitter ordeal to her; and to her kind uncle's observant eye it was evident that the girl was love-sick, but time he knew would cure all that.

We have shown by her treatment of the hapless Mary Lennox that Lady Wedderburn was neither an unjust nor unkind woman. The presence of her son in the field, and the obvious risks he ran there, led her, unlike Lady Ernescleugh, who was immersed in the gaieties of London, to turn her attention to works of charity and benevolence, even more than was her wont; to schemes for the amelioration of the poor; to schools, emigration, little allotments of land on the estate—for her husband denied her nothing; to teaching, visiting the peasantry and so forth, a system which soon caused her and Gwenny to be idolized at Willowdean, for she felt when doing all this good as if she gave hostages to Heaven for her son's safety.

Like every one else who had friends in the

army of Lord Raglan, the Wedderburns were
kept on the rack of keen expectancy during all
that memorable week which ended the month of
September. Even in mighty London every kind
of business gave place or became secondary to
this anxiety and anticipation. All knew that
the allies had landed at Eupatoria, and all cal-
culated to a nicety the day on which a battle
must be fought—a battle in which the dearest
and best-beloved of many might fall.

But it was not until the morning of the tenth
day, *after* we won the Alma, that faint rumours
through mercantile sources were heard in London, and with that evening came the telegram
which announced the total defeat of the Russians,
and that again, as in the glorious wars of old,
our arms had been victorious!

By the following day (Sunday) it was known
in Scotland, and in remote places where no
electric wire could flash the intelligence; for a
whisper seemed to pass over all the land — a
whisper which at first was full of exaggerations
and mistakes, but it found an echo in every
heart, from the apple bowers of Devonshire to
the storm-beat isles of Orkney—a whisper of the
great battle that had been fought in the strange
land so far away.

More keen and agonizing now became the
expectancy. Lady Wedderburn thought of her
son; Gwenny of her lover Horace,—wounded or

dying; yes, it might be dead and buried afar off
in that hitherto almost unknown land, so far as
we were concerned, and the names of the places
in which sounded so strange to the ears of those
at home. That already all might be over for
ever, was the haunting thought that wrung the
aching heart of each.

Three days more passed ere Lord Raglan's
telegraphed account of the battle in the *London
Gazette* reached the secluded little town in the
Merse; and with a hand trembling Sir John un-
folded the morning paper which Gervase Asloane
had taken from the despatch box, while Lady
Wedderburn and Gwenny quitted their places at
the breakfast table, and drew near him with
their faces pale and their eyes so full of eagerness and fear that an expression of expostulation
escaped the calmer Robert; and even the white-
haired butler, and the stolid and bewhiskered
footmen in plush, paused to listen for intelligence.

Skipping all the details, Sir John glanced
nervously and hurriedly through the paper,
seeking first the casualty lists of the battle; and
after running his eye down the regimental numbers, he suddenly exclaimed—

"Kate—Kate! oh, my God, our poor boy!"
and crushing up the paper, buried his face in his
hands.

While both Lady Wedderburn and Gwenny

burst into tears, fearing the worst, and a cry of terror escaped little Miss M'Caw, Robert quietly spread out the paper and saw the fatal line which had so moved his father. It came after the list of killed :

" Royal Fusileers ; Captain Cyril Wedderburn severely wounded. Since MISSING !"

CHAPTER VI.

THE WINTER OF THE YEAR.

WHEN a little more composed they began to
consider this catastrophe in its various lights.
That he was wounded severely they could not
doubt, but that he should be *missing* was a most
perplexing and harrowing thought.*   He might
be a prisoner in the hands of the Russians; or
he might too probably have crept away, as many
did, to bleed to death and die unseen—a terrible
thought! and thus his fate might never be
known.

His pale mother had but one distinct idea
—Cyril was wounded and missing too; wounded
and suffering she knew not, and might never
know, in what fashion or degree; and her
motherly hands were not there to nurse and tend
him. Her pet boy—the apple of her eye—Cyril,
always so tender and loving to her!

---

* From the time of the first landing in the Crimea till
the capture of Sebastopol, September 8, 1855, no less than
13 of our officers, 23 sergeants, and 468 rank and file were
reported missing and never traced.

All her worst, her darkest, and most terrible
anticipations seemed to be fulfilled now—so suddenly too, in the first battle. Oh, that she
could fly to him! Oh, that she had acceded to
the Ernescleugh scheme of the yacht voyage!
Horace had escaped; but why was Cyril missing?
Horace could, should, and *must* know all about
it. And, as she wrung her hands she thought,
amid all the luxury and splendour of her home,
how futile it was to reckon on earthly joys, they
were at best so fleeting!

Then as she looked over the lists and saw how
many other mothers must be suffering even as
she then suffered, she prayed for strength and
calmness to bear her cross; and prayed too as
only a mother can do, who yearningly supplicates
for her son's safety and cure.

A few more anxious days and the same des-
patch-box which has already figured in our story
contained tidings from the seat of war—the letter
from Horace to Gwendoleyne Wedderburn. It
simply announced that we had won a great
victory; and then detailed the mode in which
Cyril had been wounded.

This added anger, even an emotion of rage, to
the grief of his mother on learning that he had
fallen when performing an act of mercy and
compassion. How bitterly in her heart she
thought of that treacherous Russian! If her
son should indeed die of the wounds his hand

inflicted, the malediction of a sorrowing mother
would follow his assassin to the grave! Never,
never would she forget or forgive

" The deep damnation of his taking off."

For Gwenny's behoof Horace could not resist
saying a little about himself :

" I had a narrow escape from a shot, nearly
the last fired by the Russian artillery. I was in
the act of closing up the ranks of my slender
company (Probyn by this time was killed), when
a *round black spot* caught my eye. I knew what
it was by instinct, Gwenny ; for I had heard it
said by old soldiers, that you can never *see* a
cannon ball unless you are in its line. I threw
myself flat on the turf with a breathless exclama-
tion, and at that instant it cut in two one of my
men, and his covering file also. I felt the wind
of the shot as it passed over me !

" We are eager to attack Sebastopol before the
fortifications are increased, as they are sure to
be if any more delay ensues; and when they
echo to the drums of the British Grenadiers, the
latter will prove better arbiters than those absurd
Quaker fellows who lately tried the peace-at-any-
price dodge with old Nick, the Emperor. We go
in for any amount of shot and shell, risk and
danger here; we endure much more than I can
describe; but I care little how the time passes
as it is not spent with *you* at home. My very

soul seems to go with this to you—*all*," he felt himself compelled to add, " and my tears are falling on the paper, Gwenny. I know not what I write, or what I have written; I have no time to read it over, for already the bugles are sounding for the advanced guard to fall in, as we move at once when the last of the dead are buried."

And Gwenny's voice broke as she read that letter which poor Horace had penned on a drumhead, amid the harrowing carnage of the field— amid that terrible grey "acre of Russian wounded," groaning for water, tobacco, and sour-krout, while his thoughts travelled forward to the time when the white hands of her he loved would open and read it, and when her dark eyes might look so earnestly and sweetly over the lines his hand had written, perhaps drop a tear on them in secret and unseen.

" It is always of himself, and not of my Cyril he writes," said Lady Wedderburn, almost with anger ; " but continue."

" Already Gwenny," she read, " our once gay uniforms are in rags, the lace black, the epaulettes vanished. Our once splendid bands have been turned into the ranks, or are decimated by cholera and the bullet. We have no mess, and all the brilliance of military life in time of peace has gone. We are wretched and filthy, tattered, unkempt and unshaven as gipsies, or the homeless poor of London."

" He calls you simply ' Gwenny,' " said Lady Wedderburn, looking over her gold eyeglasses; " it is scarcely courteous, as I have often said you are *not* cousins."

Gwenny blushed in silence, but the blush was seen and noted too by Robert.

" He does not seem to have fallen in again with that odious fellow Chesters," said Sir John.

" Horace is frightfully vague about Cyril after the battle," resumed Lady Wedderburn, who could not but resent something in the tone of the letter; " he says that he saw him borne *towards* the boats, but why did he not see him carried on board of the ship personally? Oh, my boy—my poor boy may have died, or been taken prisoner on the way!"

" Scarcely prisoner, in rear of our lines," said Robert, sententiously.

" And if dead, dear Kate," added Sir John, in a low and husky voice, " he must have been found, and not returned as missing. I cannot understand it."

And so for a time sorrow and perplexity reigned at Willowdean, while all there waited each successive mail in hope and fear; and while letters and cards of condolence poured in from all the county, together with an address from the inhabitants of the little Burgh of Barony, signed by the bailie thereof, and an exhortation

from the Reverend Gideon M'Guffog, stuffed
with the usual stereotyped crumbs of comfort.

Though she sorrowed for Cyril, and deplored
the mystery that seemed to envelope his fate,
Gwenny nightly, and on her knees, thanked God
for the safety of Horace; but then natural
anxiety suggested the fear of what might not
have happened since that 22nd of September,
when he wrote his hasty letter on the Russian
drum, and the bugles were sounding for the
advance to the front!

On discovering the mistake in the Gazette,
Horace lost no time in telegraphing direct to
Willowdean, stating that Cyril was *not* missing,
but was in the hospital at Scutari, and was believed to be doing well. Then he further wrote
to mention that the announcement which gave
such pain to the family, was caused by his inabi-
lity to report to the adjutant who made up the
lists, that he had seen his cousin carried out of
the field by seamen, as he was busy for two
entire days with a working party interring the
dead; and now the army was before Sebastopol,
in the harbour of which, to bar all entrance, the
Russians had sunk their splendid fleet, adding
the crews, in battalions, to the strength of the
garrison.

Some endearing terms to Gwenny were perceptible enough in this letter; but his aunt felt
that she could forgive the writer out of the great
relief he gave her heart.

Cyril was safe, and, as she hoped, recovering !

The newspapers teemed with harrowing details of the war; the bombardment of Sebastopol began; the terrible slaughter of our Light Brigade at Balaclava made all Britain thrill with sorrow and enthusiasm; the two battles in the valley of Inkerman followed; the carnage of the last saw Horace a captain; but still he escaped without a wound; and then began the protracted sufferings in the trenches and rifle-pits—the horrors of the close siege during a Crimean winter.

The letters of Horace were always cheerful; but he had now learned the policy of writing them to Lady Wedderburn alone.

The winter of the year came on with great severity at home—with greater still by the shores of the Black Sea. Flights of wild Norwegian pigeons were seen on the hills of Fife and Lothian, and such are always a sign of heavy and protracted snows in the north of Europe.

It was Christmas-day at Willowdean, as it was all over God's fair world. A few friends, the minister and his wife, the Baron-Bailie, and so forth, were there; but when Lady Wedderburn saw the luxuries around her, the blazing fire, the glittering crystal, the fine linen, rich china service and massive plate, the chandelier decorated with shining holly and scarlet berries, the various courses at the table, the fish, and beef or mutton; the fowls, puffs, custards, and creams; the rich

wines placed before Sir John, after being solemnly
and carefully decanted from cobwebby old bottles
in secret binns known to Asloane only, she sighed
and thought with sorrow of her poor Cyril, lying
in his hospital bed, a wretched pallet, fed on
meagre broth or *bouillon;* and she thought too
of those who were shivering amid the mud of
the frozen trenches, or dying of cold and starva-
tion within sound of the bells of Sebastopol, or
crawling back to their huts half dead with
exhaustion, bearded, tattered, and squalid; and
where their only luxury might be a little half-
ground and half-green coffee, boiled on a wretched
fire, made of damp wood from the nearest thicket,
or the wrecks made by the great hurricane in
the Euxine.

Gwenny's astonishment when she found one
winter morning her window panes all frosted
over in the fashion of thistle leaves, was great
indeed, and she wondered if the cold was as great
in the Crimea as at Willowdean. And in common with all the ladies in the land, she and Miss
M'Caw knitted all manner of worsted things—a
labour of love for our poor soldiers.

Crisp lay the snow over all the level park, over
all the hills, and nowhere so crisp as in the
broad gravelled walks of the garden. Long
icicles hung from every cave and cornice; the
Leader and even portions of the Tweed were
frozen hard, and the linns where erst the torrent

roared between rock and scaur, were congealed and white as the beard of Father Christmas.

It was a season when the flakes lingered long on the Lammermuirs. The white snowdrops did not appear till April; and the purple lilacs and gold laburnams, the pink and white hawthorns, did not bloom till after midsummer in the woods of Willowdean; but ere that time came great events had taken place there, as well as elsewhere.

After the first month of spring, mail succeeded mail as usual from the East; but to the terror and grief of Gwenny, the letters of Horace ceased altogether, and a great horror filled the heart of the girl, lest something fatal had occurred!

On the other hand, to give joy to the soul of Lady Wedderburn, there came to her a letter from Cyril himself! He stated that at Scutari all had nearly been over with him; but he had found one of the dearest and most loving little nurses in the world; and that through God's grace and her care, he was now almost well—quite convalescent, able to ride about the streets, to have a sail on the Bosphorus, and bully the extortionate Caïquejees. Then suddenly in one letter he seemed to write in an agitated and disturbed state of mind, saying that a great grief had come upon him, and that he would not—yea, might never—return home on leave as his

mother wished and urged; but he was to rejoin
his regiment, and be "in at the death of
Sebastopol."

The silence of Horace, and the mysterious
grief to which Cyril so abruptly alluded, occasioned endless surmise and much perplexity at
Willowdean; but now spring had come, and
with it came a letter from Lady Ernescleugh,
then in England. After the usual details of the
gaieties of some friend's country-house where she
had spent much of the winter, she wrote thus :—

"The commander of my son's yacht writes to
me stating that she is quite ready for sea, and I
mean to sail with her for the East next month.
Lord Cardigan's yacht and others are now in the
harbour of Balaclava. *Will you accompany me ?*
Many officers' wives are content to endure the
discomforts of a residence at Constantinople, for
the purpose of being nearer the scene of those
terrible events which are daily occurring ; and
there, or even at Malta, letters and news will
reach one much sooner than when in England.
I am sick of London, and Ernescleugh is odious
to me without Everard. The doctors have pre-
scribed a change of scene, and I do so long to
see my my dear boy, or be near him. As yet,
thank God! he has only been slightly wounded
at Inkerman; but matters will go hard with me
if I do not bring him home in the yacht, and
his father also, from Corfu."

This letter, together with her desire to unravel the mystery of Cyril's conduct, which she attributed to a love freak for some Turkish damsel (an odious creature, who wore trousers, sat cross-legged, smoked a chibouk, and ate pilau with her fingers), together with the strange silence of Horace, decided Lady Wedderburn on travelling with her friend.

So slowly had passed the days at Willowdean, that Gwenny hailed with rapture the prospect of a change, and the anticipated voyage. To s those places towards which the thoughts and hearts of all were turned! Perhaps—oh! what joy—to see Horace himself! The girl became wild with delight. Stamboul, Varna, the Crimea, and the Black Sea should no longer be as mere names to her when she had seen and could remember them distinctly, as she did " dear Madras and papa's lovely house in the Choultry."

And so it was arranged that Miss M'Caw was to govern at Willowdean in their absence, and that Robert Wedderburn should escort them to London, whither Sir John—who was in Parliament representing some snug little English borough in the Conservative interest—had preceded them.

" My foolish Kate," he wrote to Lady Wedderburn, " in this proposed Crimean escapade of yours, you will be compelled to behold many a scene of horror you do not reckon upon !"

CHAPTER VII.

In the reference to Cyril's letters, we have some-what anticipated a portion of his story.

The steam frigate on board of which he had been conveyed, ran straight for Scutari with her freight of sufferers, whose number lessened every hour, as the mortally wounded, or those who were totally exhausted by loss of blood, expired, and were shot over to leeward, tied up in a blanket, or, more simply still, in their grey great-coats. Cyril endured great agony from his principal wound, together with an extreme difficulty of respiration, and even when awake he lay as one in a kind of dream, in the cabin gene-rously resigned to his use by an officer of the ship. At times, he seemed still to hear the din of battle in his ears; the sharp roar of the musketry, the booming of the artillery, the crash of exploding shells and rockets, the demon-like yells of the Russians, and the tumultuous cheering of our own troops as they closed in

upon them, and the cries of the wounded, as they
rolled, in their agony, and tore up the grass with
their fingers. But this was only the result of an
overheated fancy, for the only sound he heard
was the rush of the shining waves as they passed
the open gun-port while the frigate sped on her
way.

On the third day after the battle he was very
languid and weak, yet his listless eyes could see,
through the gun-port, that land was in sight.
Beautiful green hills were there, tall minarets of
snowy whiteness, great round leaden domes; and,
recognising Scutari as they neared it, he closed
his eyes wearily.

After a time, he was sensible of being lifted
on a stretcher tenderly and kindly, by the hands
of sailors, and found himself in the open air and
on a quay, with many more of the wounded,
surrounded by a staring crowd of picturesque-
looking Greeks, in scarlet fezzes, blue breeches,
and laced jackets; stolid looking Turks, with
great turbans; swarthy Arabs, Negro slaves, and
filthy Jews, with their sly, gleaming eyes and
long gaberdines; all of whom the Marine escort
put back with their bayonets, and without much
ceremony. Through this motley mob he was
conveyed, past the magnificent pile of buildings
which an Italian architect constructed as a
barrack for the Turkish troops (but which was
then full of our own convalescents), to the hos-

pital, which was filling fast with wounded, as
ship after ship arrived from the shore of the
Alma with her human cargo, in the shape of
mangled, emaciated, moaning, and quivering un-
fortunates, in uniforms that became rags, sodden
and saturated with mud and gore; and they were
laid side by side in the wards, pell mell, many
of them on the bare floor, where, through want
of sufficient attendance, the atmosphere soon became tainted with the horrid odour of undried
blood; causing the shocked onlooker to long for
the day—if it will ever come—when the shedding
of it should cease, and " when war shall be no
more."

The name and rank of each man, together
with the number of his regiment, were asked, as
the patients were borne in. Some could reply to
all that was required of them; but many a poor
fellow was past utterance, and could only gaze
with listless and lack-lustre eyes at the questioner,
who would enter him in the hospital books as
" a private of the Seventh Foot," " corporal,
Twenty-third Fusileers," or the " Guards," or
" Cameron Highlanders," and so forth.

Thus they were carried in, in too many instances to die unnamed and unknown, by their
fate recalling the touching lines that appeared in
a periodical :—

" Into a ward of unwhitewashed walls,
   · Where the dead and the dying lay—

Wounded by bayonets, shells and balls—
Somebody's Darling was borne one day.

" Somebody's Darling ! so young and so brave,
Wearing still on his pale, sweet face,
So soon to be hid by the dust of the grave,
The ling'ring light of his boyhood's grace.

" Somebody wept when he marched away,
Looking so handsome, brave and grand ;
Somebody's kiss on his forehead lay ;
Somebody clung to his parting hand."

Cyril's room was in a lofty portion of the
hospital, and, from a window which was near his
bed, he could see the blue Bosphorus sweeping
by the base of the dark-green mountains of
Scutari, and all the far-famed Golden Horn—
seeming such indeed, for the waters round it
were tinted with all the splendour of the Eastern
sun. And, while thinking sadly of the slaughter
that had fallen upon his regiment, and of the
faces he never more should see, his eyes gazed
with a species of vacant wonder on Constantinople, which seemed like a cluster of fairy cities
beside the strait, each a very wilderness of
shining domes, painted cupolas, gilded and red-
tiled kiosks, tall minarets, and marble fountains,
the snow-white palace of the Sultan towering
over all; the background, dark cypresses and
hills, and, in the middle distance, a forest of
masts, each bearing a flag, for the waters of the
Bosphorus were full of merchant ships, war-
steamers, swift caiques that cleft them as if

instinct with life, and shoals of glittering dolphins surging past from wave to wave.

For a time he was tormented by the groans and cries of an unfortunate young Chasseur d'Afrique, who, by some mistake, had been brought away with our wounded, and who shared his room. The left shoulder of this unhappy creature had been shattered by a large grape-shot, and the wound was perfectly incurable; but life was wonderfully tenacious within him. On the second day his ravings ceased, and turned to prayer :—

"*Sainte Vièrge, priez pour moi—pour moi!*" he would say imploringly, and then murmur softly, with quivering lips and tearful eyes, "*Ma Mère—O, ma Mère!*" in that touching and childlike spirit of devotion which the French soldier has peculiarly for his mother.

On waking one morning, Cyril found that he was alone; for the poor Chasseur had been taken to his last home, near those solemn cypresses which cast their shadows on that city of tombs, outside the walls of Scutari—the seven miles of cemetery where the followers of the Prophet lie.

For many days Cyril Wedderburn hovered between life and death, while patients poured into the hospital so fast, that the surgeons and nurses had more work on their hands than they could attend to. There was a perpetual and offensive odour of poultices, *bouillon*, preserved-meats, and jellies about the place, as they were carried to and fro; while the rending of the shirts and sheets of the dead into bandages for the living, together with the manufacture of cushions and pillows for limbs that had undergone amputation, went briskly forward in the passages and yard without.

A night of restlessness and weariness—with its occasional waking fits, during which, to the eye of the sick or ailing, a kind of phantasmagoria peoples the darkness, strange faces come of it, and fancy fills the air with odd sounds—was passing slowly away. Dawn stole into Cyril's room. The Bosphorus and all the domes and windows of Constantinople were beginning to glitter in light, as the sun rose above the hills of Scutari; and like many others in that abode of suffering, Cyril woke with a sigh, to think that another weary day of pain and inertia was before him. So faint and weak had he become, that there were times when he wished to die, and would mutter, as he lay with closed eyes—

" If I have not done much good in the world, I have not done much harm, and now I could pass peacefully away."

He was too dimsighted by the loss of blood to be able to read, even had he been supplied with books, and thus his days were days of utter weariness.

On this morning his throat was parched, and

he called feebly to the soldier who usually
attended him for water; but the soldier—one of
the Black Watch, whose left hand had been shattered by a canister-shot—did not reply, so Cyril
sighed and wearily closed his eyes again.

Something like a tear fell on his face, and
starting, he looked up, but only to shrink back
with emotions of alarm and fear, so he covered
his pale face with his thin hands.

"Cyril," said a voice, and a sob mingled with
his name. Then he trembled, for it sounded
like a voice that once had power to thrill his
heart to its inmost core.

Was it all a dream, or was he going mad?
Had the excitement of the battle, or the crash of
the bullet as it traversed his body, given his
brain a shock so rude, that sense and imagination wandered now?

No! she on whose shoulder his aching head re-
clined, whose hand caressed his now tangled hair,
whose tear had fallen on his cheek, and whose
loving, yet deep and thoughtful eyes seemed to
speak of a strange future, and of a sorrowful, it
might be awful, past, was—Mary Lennox.

Cyril had been dreaming of his mother, and
it had seemed as if her voice—the one he loved
most and best in boyhood—was murmuring in
his ear, calling him back to life; and now it was
the voice of Mary, and her soft earnest face, with
a mingled expression of tenderness and agony,
was turned towards his own.

She was very pale, rather emaciated, and dressed in a plain black costume, somewhat like that of a Sister of Charity, but without a hood.

" You here, Mary—here in Scutari—in this frightful hospital, and attending me ? Oh, explain this riddle, or I shall go mad—speak to me—place your hands in mine !" said he, huskily, in a low and imploring voice, as if he feared she would melt into thin air. But she answered, calmly—

" I arrived here, Cyril, three days ago from London, with Miss Nightingale and the staff of ladies who have come to nurse the wounded. Oh, Cyril Wedderburn, what was my emotion—my horror—when I learned that you were here !"

" Mary, it is frightful this, such work—such scenes—you will perish. Scenes of utter horror and affright ! What madness brought you here ?"

" It was no madness, but the prompting of my own heart, Cyril—a light that came to me from Heaven above, and the hope that I might be nearer—you; and now, now, oh my God !" she suddenly exclaimed, while placing her interlaced fingers on her forehead, and looking wildly upward; "after all the sufferings, the terrors, and sorrow I have undergone; after all the most unmerited shame that was put upon me; after enduring all the emotions of love, desertion, and despair, have I met you, but to see you thus—dying perhaps ?"

That Mary should have accompanied Miss Florence Nightingale—a young lady of good family, whose benevolent occupations fully qualified her for that remarkable and romantic undertaking, which made her and her trained nurses the idols of our soldiers, whose sick-beds they soothed, and whose pains and anxieties they did so much to console—fully explained to Cyril the reason of her sudden and most unexpected appearance in the Hospital of Scutari; but we leave their subsequent conversation to explain how she escaped the death to which, when last we saw her, she was hastening.

Miss Nightingale and her ladies were as ministering angels in the terrible wards of that hospital; and to the death-drowsy ear of many a wounded and sinking soldier there, how sweetly came the prayers and words of comfort they uttered in his *native* tongue.

CHAPTER VIII.

" Oh, Cyril," said Mary, in a low and earnest voice, and in her forcible way, after the first emotions excited by their sudden meeting had subsided a little, " I have undergone much that might have made my poor father's bones turn in their grave, by reason of my exceeding misery ! Though young in years, I am old in suffering : for in my brief time I *have* endured much."

" My poor Mary !" exclaimed Cyril, gazing with love and admiration on her pale beauty, which in its calm patrician style, consorted ill, or oddly at least, with her plain black stuff dress ; " tell me all that has happened since last we met."

" Since last we parted so unhappily, you should say, Cyril."

" My darling, tell me all !"

Then she briefly narrated her story up to that time when in despair, and in an evil moment, overcome by shame and terror, she threw herself into the river, and a cry of horror escaped the listener as he struck his hands together; but she had been providentally rescued by a waterman, and conveyed to a London hospital in a raging fever.

Cyril, who had listened to her in sorrow and commiseration, closed his eyes for a moment, and said in a hissing voice, through his clenched teeth—

"Oh, Chesters, there is a terrible account to be closed one day between you and me, and close it *shall*, if lead and powder avail men yet in their wrath and vengeance! The rascally affair of the drugged horse—my beautiful bay hunter; the foul cheating at play; the attempt to disgrace you, my sweet Mary, at home and elsewhere; poor Horace too in the transport—all, all make up a heavy score indeed, to be cleared between Ralph Rooke Chesters and Cyril Wedderburn."

"I was at first ungrateful enough not to thank Heaven for sparing my life," said Mary, "when I slowly recovered and the fever passed away. I was very, very weak, Cyril, and the professional politeness or conventional kindness of the hospital doctors and the hired nurses proved cold, hard, and unsoothing. I longed for the clasp of a friendly hand; for the glance of an affectionate eye; for a shoulder whereon I could lay my poor head and be at rest. Cyril, alas! you were far away—you were no longer mine—and I felt myself lonely—oh, so lonely in the world!

I have endured and felt the bitterness of death when I sinfully sought it; but not more bitter than what I endured on losing you."

"Do not heap ashes on my head, I implore you, Mary."

"In that hospital I recovered, yet only wished to die, for it seemed better, holier, purer, and every way safer to die then and be at peace, than to live and struggle on, friendless and hopeless; and yet Chesters had artfully said such terrible things of the dead who die in such places, unknown and unclaimed, that my heart shrunk within me. But one day there came a lady, with a comely face and pleasing manner—a lady who seemed to take a great interest in me, who talked to me kindly and consolingly, whom I kissed, and who actually permitted me to press my thin, wan cheek to hers—yes, even to nestle on her breast, while I told her all my hapless story. Then she took a deeper interest in me—a lonely girl without father or mother—and spoke much of the good works one may do in this world.

"Prior to her coming, I had sometimes in my heart rebelliously questioned the justice of God in creating creatures such as I, only for trial and sorrow; but she taught me that these thoughts were evil, and that I had no right to consider His reasons or purpose for chastening me. Then she spoke of her own mission, and said—

"'Come and be one of us in the East, where

we are going to nurse our poor soldiers. Our hands are weak, but our hearts are strong and true.'

" I immediately agreed to be one of these good Samaritans, and *then* I thought myself at peace with God, the world, and—myself.

" 'I have been so long the nurse of my poor papa,' said I, 'that I shall be useful, I trust. I owe God some atonement too, for what I attempted— to rush unbidden into His presence !'

" The desire to devote myself to the cause of suffering humanity became an enthusiasm within me. Existence and its personal interests seemed to have lost all value to poor Mary Lennox. I had learned to feel that out of all grief we may attain to a nobler state of life than that of the world, and as I cherished these emotions, I felt myself growing better, holier, almost sublime, in my longing to do good. I have read that ' it is well for us to remember that we are only travellers and wayfarers on this earth ;' but sometimes it seems a little hard to think how few traces of our footsteps we leave behind us when the journey is finished."

" And these emotions and purposes brought you to this horrible Scutari? To nurse all kinds of fellows, with all manner of wounds and dreadful diseases incident to camp and field ?"

A little colour came into her face as she replied—

"Yes, Cyril; and perhaps a lingering desire, or hope, to be nearer you; for though you had cast me off so cruelly, I felt that you were still—the husband of my heart. I did not desire to meet you because—because—but God has willed it otherwise. It is enough! I resolved by doing good to consecrate to Heaven the life I had so wildly, in my despair, attempted to take away."

"My poor Mary! my poor Mary! my own love!" moaned Cyril.

Her voice was grave and sweet; even so was her soft, pale face, as she replied, meekly—

"You have no longer the right to love me, Cyril Wedderburn."

"Mary?"

"Your wealthy cousin——"

"She is engaged to Horace Ramornie!"

"And you never loved her?"

"Never! I have had many a flirtation, Mary, but never loved woman save you!"

"Chesters told me——"

"Chesters again! Curses dog his steps!"

Mary said nothing more, lest she might agitate him, and while her heart began to beat happily, and even some colour mantled in her cheek, she could not but recall that painful interview, when Lady Wedderburn, by her silence, seemed tacitly to admit of his engagement with that terrible and dreaded cousin!

"Oh, my Mary, my own!" said he, while

caressing her hand, "such joy it is to hear your voice again—to feel your hand in mine. But your engagement-ring——?"

"Is gone, Cyril. It was taken from me after I was picked up senseless in the water, as I have told you."

"I will soon replace it, darling, by one that shall never be taken off your finger in life or death! I begin almost to believe in magnetic influences—in Mesmerism, and the Odic force."

. "Why?"

"For never did the touch of a human hand thrill through me as yours does, dearest Mary. Now, why is this?"

"Because I love you!" she answered, with a beautiful smile.

If it be true that "to people who are in love each casual meeting is a new miracle," in which they fancifully see the finger of fate, or destiny, or the hand of Heaven itself, how bewildering to Cyril Wedderburn was this sudden reunion with Mary Lennox!

"The past is gone for ever," said he, after a happy pause; "let us forget it; but the present is ours yet, Mary darling—my wee heather lintie," he added, sliding into the idiom of his schoolboy days; "my cushat doo, that has come all the way from the purple Lammermuirs to be my nurse and guide."

"Now you must not speak more, dearest

Cyril. Already you have said too much," said
Mary, drawing back from his extended arms.

Cyril was becoming flushed and excited, and
it was fortunate that the arrival of the staff-surgeon, Dr. Riversdale, caused Mary to withdraw to
another ward.

From that day Cyril's progress towards convalescence was marvellous; and to get chicken
broth, arrowroot, calf's-foot jelly, and an occasional glass of wine from Mary's pretty hand,
was marvellous too! Clever, versatile, full of
expedients, she made an excellent nurse, and was
adored by the soldiers, though they soon discovered that her chief favourites were the wounded
of the Royal Fusileers.

Their separation, quarrel, and sorrow; time,
and their singular isolation in that remarkable
place, made his love keener, stronger, and more
tender than ever. Glory had suddenly become
a myth and a sham! He had fully earned his
war medal, if the army was to have such a deco-
ration; he had acquitted himself as a soldier at
the passage of the Alma, as he had already done
in India. He had a fair claim for sick leave, prior
to selling out, without the hollow pretence of
" urgent private affairs;" and leave he should have,
and bring home a bride with him to Willowdean!

And in sketching out this joyous programme,
he quite forgot any scheme for the exposure or
punishment of Chesters.

Cyril saw it all—that happy future. All doubts cleared away, and Mary's wrongs atoned for, by the devotion of a life to her!

As he grew towards convalescence, however, he saw less and less of Mary. The rules laid down for her guidance as a volunteer nurse, the amenities of society, and proper policy alike required that she should only visit him at stated times, especially after he became well enough to ride about Scutari, to visit Chalcedon (and linger in the beautiful garden and plantain grove of Haider Pacha), remembering he had read in his school-boy days, that Pliny had called it "the City of the Blind;" or to ride up the eastern shore of the Bosphorus as far as Asia, and once by the daily steamer to the Islands of the Princes, to see the tomb of Irene, and other places set forth in his "John Murray."

He was intensely anxious to get well, that he might put his plans in operation and remove Mary from the perilous and, as he thought them, degrading tasks to which she had devoted herself; and, as a preliminary, he resolved to place her at Misseri's Frankish Hotel in Pera, where several officers' wives with whom he was intimate resided.

But man proposes, and God disposes!

CHAPTER IX.

"THE Royal Fusileers will parade in light marching order, and in their great coats, at twelve
o'clock to-night, and march to the rear of the
Defence Works, to join the brigade of Sir Colin
Campbell, in his *reconnaissance* of the enemy's
lines. Officers commanding companies to see
that the men's ammunition is completed to sixty
rounds."

Such was the Brigade Order read by Horace
on the evening of the 20th February; and he
muttered, "Great coats, · by Jove! I should
think so ;" for the atmosphere was bitterly cold,
and the unexpected parade was annoying, as he
had provided a little supper in his hut; and being
popular in the division, to say nothing of the
regiment, his guests would be sure to come, each
bringing his own knife, fork, and spoon; and to
some such social gatherings they had sometimes
to add their own " grog and prog ;" for before
Sebastopol an entertainment was somewhat of a

scramble, so far as viands and table appurtenances were concerned—a wretched picnic, with a perpetual shot-and-shell accompaniment.

Horace, with the assistance of the Fusileer, his servant, had contrived to make his hut pretty comfortable, and felt extremely loth to quit it on the night in question.

He had constructed an arm-chair out of an empty flour-cask, by sawing off the half of one side to the middle thereof, and therein he took his repose, and enjoyed a " quiet weed" after the fatigue of the trenches, or having a few hours' shooting behind a sand-bag in the rifle-pits, while Beamish and others who might drop in had to perch themselves on his " overland" or bullock trunks. But to turn out for a night march in the then state of the thermometer, when he expected guests, and was getting his bedfellow heated, was a decided bore—-the aforesaid " fellow" being a sixteen-pound shot which he was wont to warm in the fire by which his supper was cooked, and place thereafter at the foot of his camp bed.

Rearward of his hut the wind was howling up from the valley of Inkerman, where the graves of those slain in the two battles lay under the winter snow ; it came into the hut by many a crevice and cranny, together with a cloud of white drift whenever the door was opened, so that his candle end, which was stuck in a horn lantern, was often on the point of extinction.

The swords of Probyn, Bingham, and two other poor fellows who had fallen, were hanging on the wall until Horace could get them transmitted home to sorrowing parents or friends. A few Russian muskets and leather helmets gleaned up from the adjacent field (to be sent as trophies to Willowdean), with a bucket, some black bottles, full or empty, tins of preserved meat, a few cooking utensils, with a truckle camp bed, formed the entire furniture of Horace's abode, which measured some ten or twelve feet each way, and might have passed for the wigwam of Robinson Crusoe; but to see stray numbers of *Punch*, the *Illustrated News*, and monthly " Army List" would be an anachronism there.

The first who arrived was Everard Home, the Master of Erneslcugh, from the Guards' camp; then came Beamish, young Hunton of the 34th, Ned Elton, limping after his wound received at the Alma, and two Cavalry men; but save their swords and belts, little trace of regimentals (that good old word which is now going out of fashion) could be found upon them. All wore fur-trimmed overcoats of different kinds, caps with ear-covers, and huge warm gloves and mufflers, comfortable knitted things, the offerings of fair friends and tender-hearted Englishwomen, far away at home; and all were thickly coated with snow.

" Welcome, Ponsonby, though the last," cried Horace to one of the Dragoons; " but you can't close the door too quickly."

"True for you," added Beamish; "that intrusive beast Boreas blows the snow in everywhere."

"I wonder what Beau Brummel would have thought of such 'damp strangers' as you?" said Horace, laughing, as they shook the snow from their caps and outer garments.

Alas! now for those who had been particular in their toilettes, who were careful in parting their hair, in the choice of colours for their cravats, and were puppyish in the tint and fitting of their gloves and curve of whisker! In aspect all had become ragged and wolf-eyed, like desperadoes, and were no way ashamed of seeming so, for each made the other's costume a source of jest, and the cleverness with which he patched his own a boast.

Men who had been of the "best style" in London, and should be so again if spared; the Brahmins of Society, the Flower of the Lady's Mile, the pinks of the Household Brigade, now frequently appeared in clouted boots and strange garments of their own stitching. Their dainty straw-coloured or lavender kids had given place to worsted muffatees and mits, cut out of old forage caps, and the waxen heath blossom at their button-hole, like the delicate exotics that accompanied it, were all things of the past.

Handsome fellows who had made many a white bosom flutter and many a beautiful eye grow brighter in Belgravia, and who had hitherto given much of their spare time to the cultivation of their whiskers, and staring through the plate glass of a club-room window, were now reduced to grease their own boots, thankful if they had the grease to do so, and glad to boil their own coffee, thankful if they had the coffee and the fire to boil it; while Sybarites, who whilom had lisped slightingly of pale sherry, because it was " corked," condemned mess-room port, and talked largely of vintage wines, had now to content them with a mouthful of burning raki out of a wooden canteen, or of Jamaica rum, the gift of a casual man-o'-war's-man.

And such were the condition and aspect of those who assembled in the hut of Horace Ramornie on this night of the 20th of February; but all were lively, laughing, full of pluck, and only sorry that *their* regiments were not detailed to join in the *reconnaissance*.

" A devil of a night to go though !" said Elton. " Are we to be joined by the French ?"

" Yes; Bosquet and Villenois come with four thousand men," replied Home, the Guardsman.

" And Colin Campbell's force——"

" With your corps, will muster about eighteen hundred bayonets."

" There are some dragoons of the Turkish Contingent going under that fellow Chesters," said Hunton.

"A scoundrel who is knave enough to cheat the 'cutest fellow in the Scottish Law List—and that is a strong one," added Horace, aside to him.

His servant had by some means provided an ample supper of ham and eggs, the savoury odour of which filled the hut; to this was added a little pie of larks, which the Zouaves were in the habit of shooting and offering for sale. When these viands were discussed, cigars with brandy-and-water became the order of the night.

"By Jove! your cookery does you credit, Ramornie," exclaimed Home, who was seated on an inverted basket, with his plate on his knees. "My fellow is clever in his way too. He made a mess for me yesterday out of a slice from a goat 'found dead,' that Lucullus might have smacked his lips on tasting.

"Had Lucullus been ass enough to come here," grumbled a cavalry officer, "and not *do* 'Banting.'"

"It was quite an Apician meal."

"A truce to your classics, Home," said Horace, "or I shall fancy myself at Sandhurst again; and, in truth, I'd rather be before Sebastopol."

"You here in the Crimea, Home?" said a dragoon, suddenly recognising the half-disguised Guardsman.

"By Jove! I wish I was anywhere else," replied Home; "we last met at Maidstone, I think?"

"Are you detailed for the trenches to-night?"

"Yes; at twelve o'clock we go to the front."

"I have not seen you, Ponsonby," said Horace, "since the Balaclava day. By the way, how did you feel in the Cavalry charge?"

"Feel!" exclaimed the dragoon officer, as he tipped the ashes off his cigar, and his eyes sparkled; "I felt as if impelled on, and on, and onward by some new and terrible impulse that amounted to mad exultation—the impulse to ride over, bear down, cut, thrust, and hew, to annihilate man, horse, and everything! Our Colonel led us nobly till we were in the heart of that Russian horde, and then he fell, crying—

"'Cut your way back, my lads; go through them again like bricks; they are only Cossacks, mounted on wretched screws!'

"But three of these Cossacks pinned the fallen man to the earth with their lances, for thus he was found by some of Scarlett's Brigade, when the heavies went in for work."

"Any more news of that spy, who has figured so often among us as a Captain of Zouaves?" asked Beamish.

"No; there is a sharp look out kept for him, but he seems to be a very ubiquitous personage."

7—2

"It's in luck I am," said Beamish, "having a supper like this, after actually eating a dinner to-day."

"I dined on nothing particular," said Ponsonby.

"But I had a veritable dinner, bedad! and it is not every man who can make that boast before Seblastherpoll, as my servant Barney calls it. By the merest good luck I found a Turk lying dead, and in his havresack a chicken and a bottle of sherry—the forbidden of the Prophet. I have left only the bones of the one and the cork of the other, and did so with regret."

"Had you thoughts of swallowing them too?" lisped Ponsonby, who, though tattered and un-shaven, still retained something of his "man-about-town" air.

"What was going on at the left attack last night, Hunton? There was an awful shindy made with those two Lancaster guns in your quarter."

"Can't say, Horace; I was fast asleep—worn out. Never heard it, in fact. Besides, we are so used to the incessant pounding with those heavy cannon."

"Any word of Wedderburn from Scutari?" asked Beamish.

"Getting rapidly well, and going home on sick leave."

"The wounding of him by that Russian was a rascally affair!"

" There goes the warning bugle for our fellows !" said Horace, as the notes of the signal rose and fell on the fitful wind, and he proceeded to invest himself in a thick overcoat. " I must leave you here to finish the night as you like—only please don't burn the hut down. House property is valuable here; and there is one more bottle of brandy in the corner."

" I'll finish what I have here," said Beamish, with a sigh of regret, as he drained a bottle beside him ; " for who among us can be sure of coming back again ? The drink is uncommonly good. Who's your confiding merchant, Horace ?"

" A Sutler at Balaclava—oddivee : he writes it in his accounts. There's the bugle again, the men are falling in."

None would remain behind ; all were intent on watching, if possible, the *reconnaissance*, and so all rose to quit the hut together.

" By Jove ! Horace, in such an atmosphere as this-——"

" What—of frost, Beamish ?"

" No, tobacco : it *is* mighty difficult to find the door of your—bungalow."

" If he doesn't think himself in India again, and the thermometer twenty degrees below the freezing point. Hope you feel warm, Pat ! What an imagination you have !"

" But an utterance getting thick and feathery,"

replied Beamish, who had imbibed more than
sufficient of the cognac.

"What *are* you about?" asked Horace, laughing heartily.

"I am searching the wall in vain——"

"For what?"

"That orifice popularly known as a door."

"Here it is, and, by jingo, a soberer with it!"
cried Horace as he opened it, and the keen fierce
blast of hail and snow came in together. Giving
his arm to Beamish, whose steps were unsteady,
Horace set out for the muster place.

"Good-bye, Beamish," cried Ponsonby. "Look
me up to-morrow, if you escape to-night."

"All right; I'll put Balaclava on my visiting
list. Steady, eyes front," hiccuped Beamish,
as he floundered on through the blinding drift,
clinging tenaciously to Ramornie's arm. "Well,
if we don't leave footprints in the sands of time
before Sebastopol, we'll leave some in the snow;
but, d—n it, don't it look very like madness in a
parcel of fellows in red coats going out in the
snow to pot a set of other fellows in grey or green
coats, when all might be comfortably in bed beside their wives, if they had them."

Horace thought of his cosy sixteen-pound shot,
and laughed—some thoughts of Gwenny came
into his mind too, as they stumbled on. Gwenny
would doubtless be fast asleep then, with her
soft cheek on her laced pillow in her pretty room

at Willowdean, and dreaming, perhaps, of him, with one of the last batch from " Mudie" lying at hand.

" Are those two stars West Inkerman Lights ?"

" There is but *one* light, Pat; and no wonder that we see it so well beyond the river : it is four hundred and two feet high."

" There go the ' whistling dicks!' "

Some cannonading was going on at the right of the French batteries, which were shelling— even in such frightful weather — the earthen works that lay between the South Fort and the Quarantine Bastion ; thus, the bombs which in daylight were discernible like black globes soaring through the air, now seemed like meteors of brilliant fire, as each described an arc to the spot where it was expected to spread destruction and death.

They could hear the church bells of Sebastopol, tolling midnight, as they trod on.

The Fusileers were soon under arms, the battalion " told off," and the march began through the darkness and drift along the left bank of the Tchernaya and beside the aqueduct which had been destroyed by the Allies. The night was intensely gloomy and the snow fell heavily, impeding the progress of the regiment, which, however, successfully joined the force of Sir Colin Campbell on the high open ground which lies

two miles and a half westward of Tchorgoun, and
then there occurred that which, for a time, appeared to be an indecisive halt.

"One might live to the age of those old fellows who figure in the Pentateuch, and not
endure what we do here before Sebastopol!"
said Ned Elton, who felt his wounded limb
aching in the cold.

"What the deuce is wrong? Why are we halted
here?" asked his father, Sir Edward, impatiently,
of an aide-de-camp who trotted slowly past in
the dark, looking like a white phantom in his
coating of snow.

"There's some infernal mistake," was the
reply. "The French have not come up, and the
Russians are in great force—five thousand men
at least — in Kamara, under General Prince
Galitzin."

"The French seldom fail us."

"A messenger from General Canrobert to Sir
Colin Campbell has stated, that in consequence
of the extreme severity of the weather to-night,
the regiments he had under arms to take part in
the *reconnaissance* have been ordered back to
their tents; but the messenger lost his way in
the snow. He was too late to inform the fiery
old Highlander, who was already on the march,
and here we are!"

"And here a few of us are likely to remain,
if the halt lasts long," added Sir Edward, for the

cold was intense, and many cases of frost-bitten noses and fingers were occurring in the ranks.

Notwithstanding the state of the weather, old Sir Colin was all on fire to have a brush with the enemy under Galitzin; and it happened, as he thought, fortunately, that General Villenois, having learned that his leader's change of plans had been communicated too late, got his Zouaves under arms, and amid the dark and the snowy tempest, had moved down from the heights to join in the expedition.

A cheer from the Rifle Brigade and Royal Fusileers greeted the two dark columns of the French when they were discerned moving through the gloom; and after a brief consultation between the Generals, the command "Forward" was given, and the advance began towards Tchorgoun and Kamara at four in the morning, with the Rifles and Highland Light Infantry extended in skirmishing order.

A few cavalry of the Turkish Contingent, under Major Chesters, who had now recovered and joined the army, hovered on the right flank. The river Tchernaya lay on the left.

The orders of Sir Colin were, that not a shot was to be fired, even if they came upon the enemy, as he hoped a body of them might be surprised and quietly attacked by the bayonet; but the snow-flakes fell so thickly, that the extended files had difficulty in keeping each other

in view, and the fingers of the men were so
benumbed that very few could fix their bayonets!

In profound silence—for the tread of the
marching columns was completely muffled, even
as their appearance was hidden by the snow—
they proceeded thus, till suddenly there was a
half-stifled shout!

· Three Russian advanced sentinels had been
taken by the skirmishers of the 71st Highlanders, who literally stumbled against them
in the obscurity.

" Flash, flash! bang, ping! There go the
carbines!" cried Beamish, as the Cossack Vi-
dettes of the picquet at Kamara began firing at
random in the dark; and then followed the
hoarse din of the Russian drums, as their Infantry
began to get under arms in the town.

The order was then given to retire, for the
reconnaissance was a failure, and Sir Colin—by
the absence of Bosquet's troops—had no supports
to fall back upon in case of being vigorously
attacked; besides, the snow was falling more
heavily than ever. " One company could not
see its neighbour; each regiment was hidden
from the other, and the men were becoming,
momentarily, less able to advance." Then the
cases of frost-bite were increasing fast, especially
among the Highlanders, who had been ordered
to take off their warm fur caps and resume their
plumed Scottish bonnets.

A few random volleys were exchanged, and

then the retrograde movement began with speed. Horace was earnestly wishing himself back in his hut, and surmising that his sleeping partner, the sixteen-pound shot, would be cold enough by that time.

"We can't be back to camp sooner than midday now," said Beamish. "We have a horrid road to march by—the road that leads to glory and Sebastopol. Bad cess to both of them! Have you a drop of anything in your canteen, Horace?"

Ere Ramornie could reply, the power of speech seemed to pass from him. He received a dreadful blow in the back, and fell on his face among the snow. The entire regiment seemed to vanish from his sight, and he found himself left alone; for a half-spent shot had struck him in the back, and in the darkness, drift, and confusion, his fall was unseen, as he had been in rear of his company, which was covering the rear of the battalion.

An emotion of despair at the prospect of being left there to perish, made him stagger wildly up; but all trace of Campbell's force, and of the Zouaves of Villenois had disappeared. Nothing was visible around him but whiteness— a sheet of snow beneath his feet, and white flakes falling blindingly aslant on the biting wind that came in fierce gusts from the Black Sea.

To advance was as perilous as to retreat; for

he might be staggering towards the enemy, and
to remain still was impossible.   But his difficulties were soon solved, as he stumbled against
a party of Russian soldiers, who were already in
possession of a prisoner, a mounted officer.

To these he was fain to surrender himself,
and escape being butchered, as he had not power
remaining to use his revolver; and he found
himself marched off towards Tchorgoun, a prisoner of war, in company with the other who had
fallen into their hands in the confusion; and
that other proved to be—Major Chesters, of the
Turkish Contingent!

CHAPTER X.

OUT of the whole army, Chesters was the last man whom Horace Ramornie would have chosen for a partner in misfortune, or in anything; and he marched along by his side, preserving a grave and contemptuous silence. Twice or thrice Chesters, who seemed in no way crestfallen, attempted to open a kind of "chaffing" conversation, by offering bets about their destination, the probable term of their captivity, and so forth. But Horace made not the slightest response. And now, as day dawned and the storm abated, about eight miles distant he could see Sebastopol, with all its tremendous batteries, its green domed churches, and lofty houses, the walls of which were white as the snow that covered all the landscape.

He could see the steamers about Balaclava, and the camps of the Allies; and of these he seemed to take a farewell glance, as he and his escort descended into the valley through which the Black River runs.

An irrepressible emotion of sadness crept over him.   When should he see his comrades or be free again ?   What account of his fate would be conveyed to Willowdean ?   Letters had informed him of the grief and consternation there, consequent to the report of Cyril's being " missing" after the Alma; but how would *his* disappearance be accounted for ? and what an amount of sorrow it would cause to Gwenny !   Ideas of escape occurred to him; but he had been deprived of his sword and revolver, and the six Ruskies who formed the escort, were fellows not likely to stand on trifles with those who were in their hands.   They had rifled his pockets, deprived him of watch and rings, and stripped the lace from the collar and cuffs of the faded uniform he wore below his pea-jacket; and Chesters was treated in the same scurvy fashion.

They were all men whose raw-boned figures indicated clumsy strength.   Their features were hard, angular, and ugly.   Their long great-coats were of mud-colour, with flat metal buttons and scarlet shoulder-straps, and their canvas havresacks contained their coarse tobacco and materials for manufacturing sour-krout, while their canteens smelt strongly of raki—the three prime luxuries of their stupid and perilous lives.

One of them, who seemed rather a good-

natured man, offered Horace a mouthful from
his canteen, and then a piece of black bread,
but it looked too like a portion of peat from a
bog, and he declined both.

But to be a prisoner almost at the commence-
ment of a war was a galling and oppressive
thought to the young man! How long might
he remain so, and what might his treatment be?
The greatest empires in the world were involved
in this mortal contest, and his captivity might
last for years—for the natural term of his life
perhaps; for at that time strange and dark
rumours were afloat in the Allied camps of the
French having found in some Tartar castles prisoners who had been gleaned up on the retreat
from Moscow, and kept chained as slaves since
then. Whether such was the case or not, it is
impossible to say now; but the idea of such a
doom being his, froze the blood in the veins of
Ramornie; and he thought with agony of Gwen-
dolcyne Wedderburn becoming—perhaps when he
and his fate were alike forgotten—the bride of
another.

A body of Russian cavalry from Kamara was
now upon the march rearward, under General
Prince Galitzin, as Horace ascertained from a
passing officer who spoke French, and behind this
force he and his companion in misfortune were
marched under a new escort of dirty and un-
washed Cossacks, who to make sure of them and

save themselves trouble, mounted the captives on two spare Tartar ponies, and tied their hands to the shaggy manes thereof.

These Cossacks were all beetle-browed, ill-favoured looking fellows, with high cheek-bones, piggish-like eyes, and wore fur caps, in colour and quality closely resembling their own beards. Their uniforms were coarse and quaint, but their arms were bright and good, and each rode with his knees up to his saddlebow, and so surrounded by forage, bags of Ghiska wheat, and other plunder taken from the poor Tartar peasantry, that little more than the head and crupper of their little horses could be seen.

They were doubtless brave and resolute men, for the copper medals stitched on their coarse green uniforms showed that they were Don Cossacks, and had faced alike the rifles of Schamyl's Circassian cavaliers, and the keen sabres of the Khirghee outlaws.

This Cossack force continued riding eastward, and ere long they were at the base of the Tchatr-Dagh, or " mountain of the tents "—a flat hill not unlike the famous Table Mountain, but all of red marble, towering above groves of large trees that were leafless then, and clumps of dark green cypresses, where many a huge eagle, and whole clouds of other wild birds, hovered in mid-air. Here they shot and roasted a few bustards, which were plucked, cooked, and eaten, without being permitted to cool—there was no time for that—and Horace and the obnoxious Chesters came in for a share of the birds; though sooth to say the drumsticks were tough enough to have been used on a drum. With these they had some *youryourt*, or sour milk and Tartar cakes, taken sans cérémonie by the Cossacks from the house of a neighbouring farmer.

The snow had disappeared now in the changeable climate of the Crimea, having melted so fast that scarcely a trace of it remained even on the bare scalp of the Tchatr-Dagh, or the grotesque-looking Dimirdji Mountain, which towered on the opposite side where the halt had been made, and which was soon to be the scene of a very dark incident.

"Alexis, Ivan," said a smart looking aide-de-camp, in the rich uniform of the Princess Maria Paulovna's Hussars—for that lady was sister to the Empress, and was proprietrix of a regiment of cavalry—" bring those two prisoners before the General, Prince Galitzin."

Then the two weary wretches who escorted Horace and Chesters, and who had just lit their short pipes to enjoy a brief whiff, started simultaneously from that dirty piece of felt on which they were squatted, and which economically serves the Cossack warrior in the triple capacity of bed, tent, and cloak.

We should have mentioned in its place, that

it was Chesters who commanded the force of
Turks that so disgracefully abandoned the 93rd
Highlanders at Balaclava, but not through any
fault of his own, as he killed several of the fugitives with his sabre in vain attempts to stay the
rest. Left behind sick at Malta by the transport,
he and his affair on board that ship had been
forgotten amid the bustle of embarking for the
Crimea, and the subsequent passage of the Alma;
so that he had been permitted to join his corps
of that peculiar force, the Turkish Contingent,
where his story was unknown, or if known,
would not be understood, and now he thought
that all his gambling scrapes and sharp play had
been forgotten, so he was little prepared for what
was before him.

And now we have to apologize to the reader
for an introduction to a very unpleasant personage indeed; but such introductions are misfor-
tunes which the historian and novelist cannot
avoid.

Apart from where more than a thousand Russian
heavy cavalry had hobbled their horses, and were
cooking, smoking, eating sour krout and drinking
bitter quass or fiery raki, some lounging at length
on the still damp grass, with their belts and leather
helmets off, for the air was steamy and moist, as
the sun had so rapidly melted and exhaled the
snow of the preceding night in mist, Prince
Galitzin and a few noisy Russian officers were

partaking of a hurried repast near the wall of a
Tartar vineyard—an erection which, from its
massive thickness, age, and height, must have been
a remnant of one of the many fortresses erected
in the Crimea during the fifth century against
the Goths and Huns.

Near it rose several of those green tumuli
which are so common over all the Peninsula,
and mark the graves of those who had fallen in
the ages of classical antiquity—old even as the
days of Mithridates.

The Prince occupied a stool beside a kind of
table, both of which had been brought from the
house of the Tartar farmer, and his brother
officers stood or lay on the grass around him,
laughing and smoking. Under a loose grey great-
coat, which was open, he wore a rich uniform of
grass-coloured green, richly laced with gold. His
epaulettes were massive, and several medals and
orders of the empire were sparkling on his
breast. He seemed rather an undersized man, with
a handsome face, having dark and sparkling
eyes, set indeed unpleasantly near each other;
his nose was hooked, with a somewhat delicate
nostril, indicating Tartar blood, and his jet black
moustachios were well and fiercely curled up.

He did not rise as the two prisoners approached
him, each with proper politeness yielding a
salute, in reply to which he simply lifted his
cocked hat a few inches; but ere he replaced it,

8---2

his face and his shorn black hair recalled at once
to the memory of Horace a former acquaintance
—the person who had figured as Captain of
Zouaves among the British at Varna and elsewhere; and the fallen officer who so infamously
pistolled poor Cyril Wedderburn after performing
an act of mercy at the battle of the Alma, where
he dragged him from under his dying horse.

In short, the notorious Russian Spy, and Ivan
Tegoborski, General Prince Galitzin, were one and
the same man!

As there are upwards of three hundred Princes
of that distinguished name in Russia, we shall
have no fear of " being called out" for mention-
ing *one* of them here; but he in question was
the poorest among them, having now only his
military pay.

The first emotion of Horace was astonishment,
and then genuine contempt, that any officer
should so far have degraded himself and his
epaulettes; next he thought of the kind, gentle,
and manly Cyril Wedderburn, and his heart
grew hot with indignation. He involuntarily
turned to Chesters, but in the face of that
person read considerable alarm and disquietude;
for *he* too had recognised a former acquaintance,
who, like De la Fosse, had a gambling grudge to
remember.

" So, Messieurs," said the Russian, coolly and
with a strange smile, " we three recognise each
other, it seems ?"

"I am sorry to say that we do," replied Horace Ramornie, haughtily, in French, which he did not speak nearly so well as the Prince; but, as a traveller remarks, "the Russians have this advantage over other nations—namely, that they are endowed with the gift of tongues, having an extraordinary facility for acquiring and speaking with a pure accent any foreign language;" yet one who can speak Russian or Chinese may easily achieve anything vocable. "Monsieur le Prince, how about the coffee, the broiled chickens, and cream tarts you were wont to get from your dear mother, in Gascony? Was it honourable to act as you did at Varna, and elsewhere?" asked the young officer, boldly.

There was a triumphant and malicious but cruel glitter in the eyes of Galitzin, as he replied, coolly—

"All plans are fair in war and love, my friend. Thanks to me, Alexander Mentschicoff knew to a nicety every bayonet and sabre you had yonder in Bulgaria; yes, and every cannon too. So now we shall drop *that* subject. You are sorry to recognise me? By the bones of all the Moschti of Russia, and by every shrine in Holy Mother Moscow, *one* here shall be still more sorry at this meeting!" and his eyes flashed like a sword-blade as they turned to Chesters. He then added, to Horace, "What is your name?"

"Horace Ramornie, Captain in her Britannic Majesty's Royal Fusileers."

Galitzin made a note of the name—" Oraz
Ramhornoff, Capitan"—in a fashion that would
have puzzled Horace's friends had they seen it
on his calling cards.

" Your companion's name I know but too
well, as Captain Chesters."

" He is Major Chesters, here at least."

" That will matter little by-and-by," was the
ominous response. " What was the object of
the sudden night march from Balaclava towards
Tchorgoun ?"

" To attack you."

" Bah! I thought so; you didn't succeed
though."

" The snow——"

" Ah, Nicholas, our glorious Emperor, was
right. Holy Russia has two generals who never
fail her—January and February! What was
the strength of your force? There were Turkish
dogs among it, I know—the Asiatics !"

" For that very reason I cannot tell. Moreover, I must decline to say more."

" I might compel you," retorted the other.

" Am I to have my parole of honour ?"

" That we shall consider elsewhere. Meantime a glass of wine with you."

" Thanks, Monsieur le Prince," and Horace,
however repugnant the pretended cordiality, felt
himself constrained to clink his glass against that
of the Prince and drink with him. After which,
the latter said—

" And now, Monsieur Chesters, for *you*."

" Shall my parole be granted ?"

" No !" was the abrupt response.

" What am I to understand by that reply and your peculiar smile, Prince Galitzin ?" asked Chesters, uneasily, for his captor was known to be at heart a savage, " but a savage of health and vigour, smoothed and shapened in accordance with the prejudices of civilized life."

" Oui ; you smiled when I lost roubles to you by the thousand. I then learned to beware of the smile of such polished villains ; but it is my turn to be merry now."

" Why, Monsieur le Prince ?"

" Because you are the loser."

" In what way, beyond being a prisoner of war, I have yet to learn," replied Chesters, with ill-assumed hauteur.

" The odd trick is against you, Monsieur."

" I am indifferent about the stakes."

" That we shall see, très bon ! Come here, you fellows !" he cried to some soldiers who were loitering near, observantly. " Throw off your accoutrements, and dig me a hole here some six feet long !"

" A hole ?" exclaimed Chesters, inquiringly.

" *A grave !*" replied the hollow-hearted Russian, smiling with his false smile and black glittering eyes.

" Have you no sense of honour ?" asked Chesters, growing very, very pale.

" Some of its kind. Quick ! deeper and deeper yet ! Throw out the earth, you accursed Asiatics !" he added, kicking one of the soldiers with his jack-boot, and bestowing upon him the most oppro-brious epithet in Russia, the name of the race which closed his order. " Ah, Monsieur Chesters, you thought that some fine day, sooner or later, you would repent of your misdeeds ; and now you have not time, ah ! ah !"

" Then, have you no compassion ?" urged Horace.

" Bah ! I parted company with that long ago," laughed the other.

" Do you actually mean to assassinate him ?"

" No !"

" What then ?" asked Chesters.

" To punish you."

" Give me pistols, and I shall fight you at twelve paces—ten, if you prefer it !" said Chesters, who gazed at him with a haggard eye.

" I don't fight with cheats or tricksters, and men who use loaded dice, and know the backs of cards quite as well as their fronts, if not better. Tie his hands behind his back, and tie his feet too !"

By this time the sharply ringing brass trumpets had sounded ; the cavalry had all mounted, and formed in quarter-distance column of troops, prior to the resumption of their march ; and it was evident that whatever was about to be *done* would soon be over now.

Chesters was all that was vile and bad, yet he was the son of a gentleman—the scion of a family long honoured in his native Merse. The Crimean air had bronzed his cheek; time, and still more, dissipation, had whitened his hair. He had done deadly wrongs to the kinsman of Horace, yet the latter looked on the impending scene with horror, and prayed Galitzin, but in vain, to be merciful.

Horace remembered that there was a local story of the prophecy of a half-crazed female gipsy of Yetholm (at whom Chesters, in his mischievous boyhood, had thrown stones), to the effect that he " would never die of a sudden death, nor yet die in his bed;" and now it flashed upon the mind of Horace; but to judge by the piteous expression of his face, Chesters put no faith in the prediction, if at that moment he remembered it at all.

A couple of dragoons had unslung their carbines and were in the act of loading, ramming their cartridges home, and returning their steel rods, with a *sang froid* that was more French than Muscovite, when Chesters, who was powerful and athletic, proud and fiery, struggled fiercely with those who sought so ignominiously to bind him. Big bead-like drops of perspiration oozed over the unfortunate man's forehead, his face was deadly pale, his lips a ghastly blue, and his usually light-coloured eyes glared with all the anticipation and the terror of a sudden, merciless, and violent death, which he knew to be inevitable, yet he could not resist the natural desire to shun it as long as possible, for at that moment life seemed dear—oh, so dear! Yet in his blind despair, he sought aid neither from Heaven nor earth.

Horace called hoarsely, piteously, and then threateningly to Prince Galitzin, who only waved his hand in contemptuous silence, and then the two Cossacks once more seized him, one administering a prod from his lance to quicken his movements, and they again mounted him on the Tartar pony, re-tying his hands to the mane thereof. They then forced him away, but, on looking back, he saw a strangely horrible scene.

In his mad terror of death, or in his utter despair, Chesters, with his clenched teeth, had seized fast the coat sleeve—perhaps the arm—of one of those who were binding him. Another dragoon on seeing this clubbed a carbine and dealt him a blow on the head, a blow which, though it inflicted no wound but only a flesh bruise, completely stunned him, and he fell senseless.

"In with him as he is and cover him up," said Galitzin, remorselessly. "Keep your ammunition for others! Quick—obey me, or it shall be the worse for yourselves!"

The two dragoons who had paused with loaded carbine in hand, now relinquished them, for they knew that Galitzin was not a man to brook delay, or have his temper trifled with; and taking a couple of Tartar shovels, they proceeded to assist in filling up the grave upon the yet living and breathing man, whom the cold earth so speedily revived that a sense of his situation dawned upon him!

A half-stifled cry of despair, that made the blood of Horace congeal, came out of that hole; another and another followed, each, however, more faint than the last, as the load of earth grew heavy upon him. Then came a sound like a convulsive groan or snort; anon it was completely filled, and they batted the heaped-up mound with the flat of the shovel. Four feet below that heap writhed the yet living man, bound hand and foot; and while the *Pulkovnick*, or Colonel of the Russian Dragoons, gave his hoarse words of command to "break into sections" and "march," while the kettledrums rolled and the trumpets pealed forth a lively and martial air, Horace, as he looked back, thought he could see the mound of earth heaving, as the strong man struggled in his death agony amid the depth of his living grave!

So thus, in some fashion, the prophecy of the revengeful Yetholm gipsy came true after all; and the onyx ring of Louis De la Fosse, with its heraldic gauntlet on a sword's point, and the motto *Droit en avant*, became the prize of an ignorant Cossack, who tore it with his teeth from the finger of the half-senseless man.

This was all base revenge on the part of Galitzin, as he was a man stained with a thousand crimes and immoralities.

So there Ralph Chesters found his grave by the ruin of an old wall of the Gothic days, and amid a lonely clump of caper-trees and juniper-bushes in Crim Tartary!

CHAPTER XI.

THE PAROLE OF HONOUR.

THE Russian troops in the Crimea were always being changed, with what object it is impossible to say; but those who were once engaged with the Allies seldom saw them again. Thus the Heavy Dragoon force of Prince Galitzin wheeled off towards Simpheropol, *en route* for the Isthmus of Perecop, while he, accompanied by his aide-de-camp and a few Cossacks, proceeded direct to Yaila, carrying with him one of the few trophies lately secured by the Russians—Horace Ramornie.

The repugnance the latter had of his captor was intense, yet he was compelled by policy to dissemble to an extent that made him almost despise himself; for he had to smile and bow his thanks whenever that personage proffered—as he not unfrequently did—his cigar-case, with a bland yet cunning glitter in his eyes. With all his bad points of character—and Horace knew not the half of them—he sorrowed for the sudden and terrible fate of the hapless Chesters, and justly

deemed his death, and more than all, the mode
of it, an outrage on humanity, on the laws of war
and of nations; for whatever their private quarrel
may have been, Galitzin should have respected
the rights of a prisoner.

But the butchery of our wounded in the Valley
of Inkerman, the massacre of a boat's crew under
a flag of truce at Hango, and the cannonading
of our ships that were perishing amid the terrible
storm that swept the shore of the Euxine, go far
to prove that the Russians are not particular in
their mode of dealing with an enemy, or remarkable for their nice notions of chivalry.

So the close of the second day, after some forty
miles march, saw Horace Ramornic a prisoner in
the Castle of Yaila.   Along the route he had
noted every path and defile, every Tartar village,
every wall and tree, that might guide him if he
succeeded in escaping.   That project, if put in
execution, had with it many perils; for he might
be shot, or shut up among the rank and file and
sent inland he knew not where!   He writhed
under the restraint of the present, and anticipated
the future with doubt and dread.

However, once within the gates of Yaila, his
parole of honour was accepted by Galitzin, as
commandant of the place, to the effect that he
should not go more than *one* mile beyond its
walls, reporting himself every night at gunfire to
the *parooschick* (a lieutenant) of the main-guard;

that he would be made a close prisoner if he failed in these conditions, and eventually shot if he attempted to escape.

Horace was fain to accept of these hard terms, stipulating, on the other hand, that his life should be safe, and that he might write to his friends at the camp by a Tartar messenger.

This was peremptorily refused by Galitzin, lest he should in some hidden terms describe the locality of Yaila and strength of the garrison; for distrust of everything and everybody was a second nature with this impoverished Prince. Moreover, he had been more than once a spy himself; so hence came much of the mystery that involved the disappearance of Horace Ramornie.

When he found himself isolated thus in that sequestered fort, amid the mountains of Crim Tartary, at times a stunned sensation came over him. He felt like one who wanders in the unknown places of dreamland, or under a species of nightmare! Was he the same Horace Ramornie who had lately so many friends, a position and rank as Captain in the Line—who had been riding between a file of filthy snubnosed Cossack Lancers, in coarse uniforms and mangy-looking fur shoubahs, with his hands tied to the shaggy mane of a stolen Tartar pony; and was he actually to pine there, under the shadows of the Tchatr-Dagh and Dimirdji Mountains, for some unnamed period of time?

If this was reality, was Gwenny a myth?

The longing to escape was intense; but then he had given his parole; and to ask it back, would be to announce the intention of flight, and cause him to be made a close prisoner, who would be well watched in one of those cells or dungeons of the place, the bare thought of which made him shudder. He could but hope that some body of the Allies might by chance assault Yaila, and effect his rescue; if the Ruskies did not bayonet him, to prevent him from falling safe into friendly hands; and *that* he knew they were quite capable of doing.

Rising from the slope of the hill, on rocks of red and white marble, the Castle of Yaila consisted of four towers of very picturesque aspect, connected by an embattled curtain, or wall, before which lay a deep ditch of recent construction; and, in its time it had witnessed many changes, and had many masters.

The basement was originally part of a citadel erected by the Emperor Justinian against the barbarians. The family of a Khan of the house of Zingis, leader of the Golden Horde, who came from the deserts of Tartary to conquer Russia, had occupied it for several generations. It had been demolished by the Genoese, when the Superb City was mistress of Lesbos, Cyprus, and "Scio's rocky isle;" and it had been restored, to undergo a cannonading by Mohammed the Second,

when he swept her industrious colonies from the
shores of the Black Sea.

Now, each of those sorely-patched round
towers, was surmounted by a Russian cupola, the
copper of which was of a brilliant green colour.
Two were shaped and striped like water-melons,
and two like pine-apples, being cut into knobby
points to make the resemblance more complete.
Each terminated in a great cross, and over all,
on the mast of a ship brought from the Euxine,
waved the white standard of the Empire, charged
with the blue saltire of its patron, the Fisherman
of Bethsaida.

The garrison (Horace, intent on rescue if he
could not escape, took note of everything) consisted of two four-company battalions of Finland
Infantry, under the *Pulkovnich,* or senior Colonel,
Alexis Tegoborski, a kinsman of the Prince—a
grim old soldier, who had lost the half of his
left hand by a Turkish sabre, at the siege of
Varna, and wore a gold medal for the war in
Transylvania. As each Russian company is supposed to be two hundred strong, this garrison
should have consisted of at least sixteen hundred
bayonets; but as Galitzin was one of those good
old-fashioned Muscovite officers who peculated
whenever he could do so, he had barely two-
thirds of that number in his ranks; but when
the (obliging) General of the District inspected
them, the rest were borrowed from the next

officer of the same school at Simpheropol, Kertch, or elsewhere; and the General, pocketing a share of the pay, said nothing about it.

In general vulgarity of appearance, as well as in coarseness of face, it was difficult to distinguish the officers from the men on parade. All wore the same long grey coat, that hid everything, to their gaiters; but under this, each had a dark-green coatee, faced with red and trimmed with yellow, like their flat, round forage-caps.

Heavy cannon, all painted green, with white crosses on the breech, commanded the approaches to the place on every side, and Horace saw with a sigh, that even if some General of the Allies suggested a sudden expedition of the troops to Yaila, as Campbell did to Tchorgoun, that the Castle would not be taken without a terrible loss of life; yet, he was fond of imagining the joy with which he would see the Red-coats, or the active Zouaves, in their baggy madder breeches, crossing the ditch under grape and musketry, and swarming up the rocky glacis at the bayonet's point. And then his heart would leap within him, only to sink lower in hope than ever. For when was it to be?

Though a Russian Prince, and, consequently, we may suppose, a gentleman, Galitzin had but vague ideas of the position held in English society by an officer of any rank: and though the superannuated nurse of the Emperor, and even

his coachman, have the nominal rank of Colonel
—for everything is judged by the standard of
the sword and epaulette in Russia—he was dis-
posed to treat the " Hospodeen Ramhornoff," as
he called him, rather coldly, and all the more so
when reverses came thick and fast upon the
garrison of Sebastopol.

So February passed into April, and wistfully
and yearningly did the prisoner gaze upon the
blue waters of the Euxine (piquancy being given
to that glimpse by the sails and smoke of our
war-steamers, cruising between the Straits of
Yeni Kale and Sebastopol), " the highroad to Old
England," which lay about two miles from his
place of detention. And his soul sickened of
the same eternal view. Yet that view was not
without its charms.

There were the stupendous peaks of the
Dimirdji and Tchatr Dagh; the picturesque little
Tartar villages with white walls and green roofs;
a peep of the wooded valley of the Salghir—the
silver rivulets stealing between the slopes of
'emerald green towards it and the sea. Groups of
passing natives ; the Asiatic women, with loose
trousers and flowing headdresses—the Russian,
with high-waisted petticoats; the turbaned and
slippered Turk, with a bundle of weapons in his
sash; a mounted Tartar, in a red striped jacket
with blue trousers and scarlet sash ; a Russian
Mujik, in jackboots and sheepskin jacket: and

troops of all arms, perpetually pouring forward
to or from Sebastopol; and high over head the
black eagles soaring in the blue sky. But
Horace sighed for his little tent in the British
camp; for his perilous tour of duty in the
trenches; for creeping towards the rifle-pits in
rear of a sap-roller; and to hear once more the
ding-dong of the great guns, night and day, in
and around the beleaguered city!

The greatest terror of Horace was a snowy
or, as the season opened, a wet day, for then he
was of a necessity confined within the walls.
Minus umbrella and wrappers, he could not even
enjoy his paroled mile, but was compelled to
keep within a dingy whitewashed room, heated
by a *peitchka* or wall stove, with a tattered copy
of the *Times* or *Galignani* three months old,
which somehow found their way there, and from
which the censor of the press had carefully ob-
literated everything of the slightest interest;
otherwise he would encounter General Prince
Galitzin, who was most exacting of salutes, at
every other turn of the old tumbledown Tartar
stronghold, every stone of which he loathed.

The weeks were marked only by a bearded
Greek priest, who performed service on Sunday
in the armoury, clad in white, with gorgeous
vestments of cloth of gold, bordered by the
richest lace.

Sometimes he had the honour of dining with

the Prince, and the pleasure of having his usual meal of beef, black bread, and beer, especially after wrecks in the Black Sea, varied by a repast *à la Russe*, where everything was excellent, from the preliminary kimmel and caviare, to the coffee that closed it. There would be turbot from the Euxine, wild boar from Khutor Mackenzie, potatoes garnished with parsley and butter, salted beef and green *borsch*, plenty of fruit from Achmetchet, and *crimskoi* or Crimean wine, and that of the Don, which so often passes for champagne in Russia.

Galitzin, to Horace, seemed then a kind of Belshazzar in a green coat and epaulettes, but discontented, and sighing for the beauties of St. Petersburg and the hells of Paris and Baden-Baden. He never asked Horace to play, however, as he knew well that the industrious Cossacks had stripped him of everything, even to half the buttons on his uniform.

On these occasions, when under the influence of the wine, Galitzin would relax a little of his stiffness, and Horace would strive to forget that he was the guest of a spy and assassin—yea, a double one (for by this time Cyril might be dead at Scutari); and once he begged " that his parole might be extended to two miles," as he had an intense longing to stand by the shore of the free rolling sea—but dared not to hint that.

Galitzin bent his keen dark Tartar eyes inquiringly upon him, and said significantly :—

"Are you ill-treated here ?"

"Monsieur le Prince, do not misunderstand me ; I simply wish to wander out to see——"

"What, Monsieur le Capitaine, if the Tchatr Dagh, the Trapezus of the Greeks and the Palata Gora of the Russians, together with the mountains of Yaila, are where they were yesterday ?"

"Well, life has come down pretty much to that sort of thing with me. To find that any of them had vanished like the Palace of Aladdin, would cause a new sensation — a surprise at least."

"An *alerte* from Balaclava would be more acceptable ?"

"Decidedly, Monsieur le Prince," said Horace, smiling.

"You weary of your imprisonment and of our Tauric scenery ?"

"How much I weary, heaven alone knows !"

"Well, empty that bottle of Donskoi; your exchange or release is only a matter of time."

And Horace thought sadly in his heart—

"Patience, patience yet awhile. What is there on the land or sea that is *not* a matter of *time ?*"

How regretfully, yet proudly, he thought of his regiment, the Royal Fusileers—of that splendid group of English officers, who gathered round the farewell mess-table at Chatham—the table that is at once the model of aristocracy, democracy, and dinner society—men so high-hearted, noble, and generous, of all those who drew their swords that morning beside the Alma; of Jack Probyn, of old Conyers Singleton whose blighted life was closed by a Russian bullet; of Pomfret, Bingham, and Joyce, and all who had fallen; of Sir Edward, Ned Elton, Pat Beamish, and others, who, he hoped, were surviving still. His heart turned to them with affectionate longing. He felt himself so much alone among all those hostile foreigners, with whom he had no community of feeling; alone with his sorrows, doubts, and harrowing fears of liberty, promotion, and more than all perhaps—a love lost!

The yearning for letters that could never come, and for news of those at home, became keen and poignant. How drearily the round of each day passed! The utter sameness of place and view and occupation, or rather lack of the latter; so that each night he thanked heaven that another day of his life had gone, and he was twenty-four hours nearer the end of his captivity.

But the *end*—when might it be?

Surmises of how the war was going on were incessantly in his mind, with thoughts of Gwenny, of Lady Wedderburn, and of their health, or where they might be, whether at Willowdean or in London, where Gwenny would certainly be the object of so much attention! Poor girl! he flattered himself that her sorrow for him would be great indeed—all the greater that she had still perhaps to keep the secret of their engagement in the recesses of her own heart.

And so while he pined thus within the narrow limits defined by his *parole d'honneur*, the soft Crimean spring stole on towards summer, and the soldiers of the garrison were changed many times. Then came the hum of the mountain bee as it floated over the little caper bushes or the purple heather of Yaila; the plash of the brown scaly fish in the stream that bubbled towards the Salghir or the sea, and these were the only sounds that broke the stillness of the lonely hours Horace spent on slopes outside the fortress (for he loathed the in), while the fertile soil around began to teem with mint and thyme, wild parsley and aromatic herbs; the great dahlias, sweet-briar, and whitethorn flourished amid the marble rocks and the crumbling walls of the days of Justinian and the Genoese, and every breeze of summer as it swept past was laden with delicious perfumes.

Meanwhile, the Czar Nicholas had died; the great sortie of the 4th of April had been repulsed; the rifle-pits had been captured; the terrible conflict took place in the cemetery;

Sebastopol still held out desperately, but the Russians were hemmed on all hands within it.

Galitzin was a great tyrant. Seldom did a day pass without finding an officer under arrest for some petty fault; or a soldier mulcted of his miserable pay for the Prince's behoof, flogged, tied neck and heels to a musket, or sent to shot drill; and these punishments generally took place in the evening, after Galitzin had imbibed his full share of crimskoi; and after witnessing them, and saying prayers before a gaudy print of his patron, St. Ivan Veliki, he generally retired to smoke a cigar in the apartments of his kinsman, the Pulkovnick Alexis Tegoborski, with whose florid and fair-haired wife, Norina Paulovna, he seemed on remarkably intimate terms.

So thus the spring wore into summer, and Horace Ramornie was still a lonely prisoner, pining in the Castle of Yaila; but new, strange, and terrible interests were to grow up around him ere he saw the last of its four green-domed towers and heavy gun batteries.

CHAPTER XII.

THE YACHT.

On the evening of one of those same summer days which Horace was spending so sadly among the green slopes outside the fortress of Yaila, a beautiful English yacht was seen standing before a fair wind between the European and the Asiatic shores, between the fortress of Karibdsche on its barren rocks, and the lighthouse of Anatali Kawak.

At this place, the narrowest part of the Bosphorus—the waters of " the Sacred Opening" —the waves seemed to be sleeping in golden light. A strong flush of splendour from the sun, then sinking towards the Thracian chain of Hæmus, fell in all its glory on " Olympus high and hoar," and all the undulations of the Bithynian range ; the purity of the atmosphere, bringing clearly to the eye the shining windows of many a gaily-painted and gilded kiosk, the marble peristyle and leaden dome of many a little mosque ; the pretty villages, the gigantic cypresses, and the beautiful groves of fig trees; the water being so transparently pure and clear, that nearly all these objects were reflected downward in its glassy depths, exactly as if in a mirror.

The yacht was a smart little schooner of some two hundred tons, straight and low in the water, and coppered to the bends with metal bright as burnished brass. She carried a vast spread of fore-and-aft canvas, which was white as snow; the masts raked well aft; the deck was flush, the only encumbrance being six small brass carronades, for ornament rather than use, though a garland of shot for them was round the coamings of the hatchways.

The elaborately carved figure-head was the effigy of a handsome woman, with flowing tresses, bearing a gilded wand, which was always un-shipped when the yacht went to sea; and now the empty hand was pointed as if directingly towards the Black Sea. The yards were light, and the spars tapered away aloft like fishing-rods; the union-jack and ensign of the Royal Yacht Club were duly displayed, one at the gaff-peak and the other at the mainmast-head in answer to the crescent and star on the ramparts of Karibdsche.

The tiny companionway, all walnut wood and brass, was like a toy staircase, and the cabin was furnished like a lady's boudoir, save that it was

hung with coloured prints of operatic favourites
and dancing-girls, in the shortest of skirts, pho-
tographs of "some fellows of ours" in the
Household Brigade, French crayon heads and
studies, some of them slightly objectionable in
character—for this was the yacht of the Master of
Ernescleugh, and that handsome girl with the
fine features so delicately pale and minute, with
dark eyes and hair, to whose fashionable costume
a piquancy was given by the dark-green Sardinian
Bersagliere plume which she wore in her little
velvet hat, and who was gazing through her
lorgnette alternately at the European and the
Asian shore, is Gwendoleyne Wedderburn.

Lady Ernescleugh and Lady Wedderburn were
below. They had been more than once to the
East before, and the Bosphorus was nothing new
to them. A heavy gale had been encountered
the preceding night in the sea of Marmora, and
they were now lying on the luxurious velvet cabin
sofas, each fanning herself, bathing her face with
Rimmel, in which a handkerchief was dipped, and
both eager for the time, when after traversing
some three hundred and odd miles of the Black
Sea, they should be able to embrace their sons.
The yacht did not anchor at Constantinople,
as Lady Wedderburn had been given to understand that Cyril had left Scutari for headquarters.

"Oh, the foolish fellow!" she exclaimed, " to

risk himself again, when he might have come home with honour !"

She was anxious that Cyril should see Gwenny as soon as possible ; not that the trenches before Sebastopol were quite the place for marrying or giving in marriage, or a Crimean hut the place wherein to spend a honeymoon ; but she had begun to have certain jealous fears of secret views entertained by her friend, the fair Ernescleugh, for *her* son, whose extravagance was boundless, and for whom the wealthy Indian heiress would prove a very seasonable match. Once, when she exclaimed in admiration—

" Oh, it is quite a fairy ship this !"

" Were my son to hear you, he would doubtless make you a present of it," replied Lady Ernescleugh, kissing her cheek. " Would you like to be mistress of it, child ?"

" Gwenny !" exclaimed Lady Wedderburn, not knowing very well what to say.

" I am so enchanted with everything, and yonder beautiful shore !"

" If the Sultan heard you, Miss, he'd likely wish to make you mistress of *that* too !" said Bob Newnham, the commander of the yacht, with an air of gallantry.

Many a day at Cowes and Ryde had the Master of Ernescleugh figured on the deck of this yacht with other guardsmen, wearing sou'westers and the roughest of Petersham dreadnoughts, with glazed boots and scarlet neckties, and with shirt collars of marvellous size and pattern, all over ships and anchors, all thinking they " were doing the thing uncommonly well;" and now he was toiling in rags in the trenches, or the occupant of a hut inferior to his dog-kennel at home, while more than one of his brother yachtsmen— poor fellows !—were lying quietly in their graves on Cathcart's Hill, or in the valley of Inkerman.

And now as the yacht bore on, careening gracefully over, when the wind drew more abeam, a breeze which, however gentle, sufficed to make the sea chafe in surf about the Cyanean rocks, Gwenny filled up her time by chatting gaily with Newnham, who, though a soured and some-what homespun character, could not but be charmed by her beauty and vivacity.

To Gwenny, secluded so long as she had been at Willowdean, this voyage to the East had been a source of uninterrupted joy. Gibraltar with all its batteries, Malta with its churches and streets of stairs, and but lately the Cyclades— Sirpho with its steep mountains, Thermia with its caverns, barren Joura (the Botany Bay of ancient Rome), Andros with its mountains covered with arbutus, and all the other " Islands of the Blest;" and then came the Dardanelles and Constantinople, her crowning wonder, for she saw only its beauties and knew nothing of its streets of mud.

A joyous and light-hearted girl of eighteen to be transported into a world of such novel sights and sounds, new scenes and tastes, new pleasures and daily excitements — more than all, to be going to behold with her own bright eyes that great beleaguered city, of which all the world was talking, thinking, or writing, where daily and nightly her mysterious—was it possible?— naughty Horace, who had ceased to write to her for so long, was facing danger—all proved a source of thrilling excitement.

Bob Newnham, the commander of the yacht, was as enchanted by her questions as she was bewildered by the utter incomprehensibility of many of his answers, for nautical terms were as Hebrew to her. He was somewhat tall for a sailor, with a fair but saddened face, in the lines of which disappointment was too evidently written. He was nearer fifty than forty years of age, quite bald, only a lieutenant R.N. yet, and never hoped to be more, even in this time of war. Poor Bob Newnham! He had neither patronage nor interest; ambition was dead within him now, and he was content to be a kind of "upper servant," as he sometimes said in the bitterness of his honest heart; for he thought the skipper of a lord's yacht was only a degree better than his butler or gamekeeper ashore, and not half so comfortable a berth as either had; and he had more than once lost his situation for threatening

to " colt," or ropesend, for their aggressive inso-
lence, some of the young sprigs and *parvenus* in
whose service he had been since he was last paid
off in Hamoaze, after long service in the horrid
Africa squadron, where he had learned too well
to know the truth of the sad rhyme,—

> " The Bight of Benin,
>   The Bight of Benin ;
> But *one* comes out,
>   When *three* go in."

Newnham was by birth a gentleman ; but he had
gone early to sea in the rough old sailing-ship
times, when steamers were stigmatized as "smoke-
jacks;" when the midshipmen's berth of Marryat's
days was not much improved since those of To-
bias Smollett ; and he had been more used to tar
and slush, than white kids and perfume, or even
a white tablecloth, " though," as he often said,
" he was obliged to affect all these sort of things
now."

Lady Eruescleugh thought his solecisms dreadful, deeming him a creature only to be tolerated
because " that absurd boy Everard rather likes
him, for they played chess, cards, smoked and
made much noisy fun together, when the former
chose to be nautical, and have a few miles' voyage
in the yacht with a few friends from London ;"
and the maintenance of the said craft, with her
crew of some twenty-two hands, all told, cost a

pretty sum annually, when added to the little brigade expenses of the Honourable Everard.

"And those little cannon, they are so beautiful and clean!" continued Gwenny, who was still enchanted with everything.

"We generally give 'em a polish on Sundays, Miss, when the men are idle," replied Newnham, who stood near her with a telescope under one arm and his hand thrust into the pockets of his reefing jacket,—a semi-uniform, as it had gilt buttons and gold lace.

"I think I could fire one myself! Would you permit me?"

"With pleasure."

"But I mean if the Russians attacked us."

Newnham laughed, and while looking down on the bright face and its wonderful long eyelashes, replied, "Thank God that, for your sake, there is no fear of the Russians attacking us, Miss. All their craft are choke full of stones, and lying low enough at the bottom of Sebastopol harbour. We are as safe here as if we were off Blackwall!"

"You would like to fight them though, I suppose?"

A gleam passed over his clear blue eyes, and the colour deepened in his cheek, as he replied, "You talk of practical fighting—I can't get the chance,—but that would be nothing to me. I am one of those luckless dogs, Miss Wedderburn,

who in the mighty battle of life have had to fight
before the mast, thankful that I could keep my
place there, and maintain myself and my poor
mother—for she is living yet.   But to fight a
Russian gunboat, however small," he added,
laughing, " and with these toy carronades, would
be exactly like scuttling a ship to get rid of the
rats—we should lose her anyway."

" And our liberty ?"

" Yes, if we did not lose our lives." .

" Oh, that would be dreadful !"

" Though there is no fear of that sort of thing ;
there are some frightful squalls at times in these
waters, and my advice to Lady Ernescleugh should
be, that as soon as she has landed at Balaclava
harbour all the good things we have for her son,
the preserved meats, cases of wine and stout,
(Rimmel's perfumes)" he added, parenthetically,
and with a peculiar smile ; " and after she has
seen him—that is, if he ain't already under the
turf, we should haul up for Constantinople, and wait
awhile there, to see what turns up in the Crimea.
The infernal work can't last much longer there.
We are to have a rough night, I fear."

" Worse than the storm of last night ?"

" Storm—bless me, Miss Wedderburn, it was
only a capful of wind.   We had the mainsail and
fore and aft foresail close reefed, to be sure, and
the sea made some breaches over the deck, wash-
ing a few buckets to leeward, but that was all ;

she went through it like a duck. Unfortunately
we were too near the Isle of Prote, and when it
blows I like a good offing and plenty of sea
room. We are not in the Mediterranean now,
and I believe (even when there) with the old
Admiral Doria, that 'its three best harbours are
June, July, and Carthagena.' It is freshening
already, by jingo!" he added suddenly, as the
lofty schooner careened over more heavily to
leeward; "and I didn't like the look of the sun,
as he went down behind the hills, looking yellow and pale at last."

"It *is* coming much stronger, sir," said the
mate, in a. low voice, and after a consultation,
and much anxious gazing at one particular quarter of the sky, where to Gwenny's amazement
nothing was to be seen; but where, with the
true instincts of seamen, they seemed to discern
much to excite solicitude.

"House those carronades alongside (we only
showed our little teeth as we passed Constantinople, Miss Wedderburn); lower away and lash
the gun ports fast, for I see that it will be a
night of close-reefed canvas again," said Newnham. And ere long the wind increased so much
that sea after sea pooped the yacht, and her commander donned his oilskins, while she rolled
fearfully on the long and heavy swell which is
so peculiar to that ocean. Gwenny was compelled to go below, and Newnham handed her

down just as the light of Faranaki-in-Asia began to glitter like a star across the darkening water, and Mount Hæmus on the opposite shore was sinking faint and blue, while the schooner bore on her course, northeastward, into the lonely Euxine, for not a sail or trace of smoke was visible as gloom and obscurity descended on the sea.

CHAPTER XIII.

FATE.

CYRIL was still full of his project — his most earnest desire to remove Mary Lennox from the perilous atmosphere of the Hospital at Scutari, and place her in the care of an officer's wife, whom he knew, and who resided in Misseri's Frankish establishment, the Hotel d'Angleterre; if not there, in the *pension* of Madame Giuseppino Vitale, so famous for the views from her windows, though that there *was* an awkwardness in a young unmarried officer procuring quarters for a young unmarried lady, he could not but admit; however, ere he had quite decided what to do, there occurred an event which he had dreaded, yet could not bring his mind to anticipate.

He had recovered with marvellous rapidity, having suffered more from loss of blood than from actual severity of the wounds inflicted by Galitzin, though that near the lung had been certainly dangerous; but what astonished and distressed him for a day or two was that Mary, who had long since ceased to attend or visit him, had entirely disappeared, and his servant, the soldier of the Black Watch, could tell him nothing about her. He could no longer meet with her light figure in its sombre dress, flitting about the passages that led to the wards, crossing the square from the laboratory or soup kitchen, and he began to fear that she had left the place for some reason or purpose known to herself alone.

Could she be ill? Alas! that was likely enough. He remembered that since he had first seen her in Scutari, she had been daily growing thinner, even as he waxed in strength and flesh. Her figure, once so fair and round, had seemed to be fading away; her cheeks had become hollow, and her white temples too. Her hands had become painfully attenuated and almost transparent, all bespeaking what some one terms " the lingering decay of the delicate physique."

Cyril Wedderburn was sorely distressed by the recollection and conviction of all this; and, blaming himself for remissness in not having her removed sooner, after three days had elapsed without seeing or hearing of her, he went forth to make inquiries.

" Depend upon it," thought he, " inspired by an emotion of false delicacy, or something of that kind, she has given me the slip and bolted for England perhaps, by the steamer from Galata."

Alas! he little knew that poor Mary had not a sixpence in the world she could call her own.

" I was anxious, of course, to get her out of this horrid place; but I hope she has not anticipated the move by any rash plan of her own," thought he; " but anything is better than being here," he added, for with something akin to terror, he had seen her hovering in the cholera wards, where the patients were in all stages of collapse, with cold extremities, rigid muscles, and faces white or blue; and yet among them she had gone cheerfully, gliding about, with her doses of opium, brandy, soda and calomel; and old Doctor Riversdale, who was now there on duty, affirmed that she was worth any dozen nurses put together.

" It is all very fine, but by Jove, a fellow don't like the girl who is to be his wife doing all that sort of thing among the rank and file," said Cyril to her one day when he expressed his genuine astonishment and grief to find her thus occupied. " It may be enthusiastic, self-sacrificing, and so forth, but it is not the work for an English lady. In the French Sisters of Charity it seems somehow altogether different, but in our Protestant folks I can't understand it."

" Oh, Cyril," she had replied, gently, " we must bear patiently—I at least have learned *that* now —and with proper fortitude and resignation, the ills and the work that Fate has marked out for us."

But Mary's frame was ill-suited for such tasks and for such an atmosphere; and now Cyril learned, with horror and dismay, from a passing staff-surgeon, that " the poor girl was down with cholera, and was in that wing where the women's ward lay; have a cigar, old fellow," he added, proffering his case, " and don't go near that place if you can avoid it."

The medical officer said all this quite in an offhand way, little dreaming that he was plant-ing a sword in the heart of his hearer, who hurried away, stunned and overwhelmed, to the place he indicated.

It was a great rambling Turkish house, which had once been the residence of some wealthy merchant of Stamboul. Some Turks were on duty that day about the Hospital, and a stolid-looking Mahommedan soldier, in his scarlet fez, blue jacket and red knickerbockers, stood sen-tinel under a sunshade, leaning on his musket and smoking a cherrystick chibouque. He started and saluted Cyril, and something expressive of astonishment that a man not a *hakim* should come to visit women, escaped him; but Cyril pushed him aside and strode in; for all our notions are reversed in that peculiar land where the ladies wear trousers and the gentlemen often petticoats; where the ladies ogle through the eyelet-holes of their yashmacs, and the gentlemen look demure and abashed; where the men wear all the gay colours and women the sombre.

An English soldier's widow who had acted as nurse there since her husband died of his wounds, soon led Cyril to the room where Mary lay— a small apartment that opened off the stately Divan Hanée, having walls painted white and the roof a flaming red, lighted by pointed windows of stained glass; and in this kiosk (a term signifying a room, or a house indifferently) she was stretched on the floor, the occupant of an hospital straw-pallet and covered by a coarse brown military rug, on which were stamped in tar, the broad arrow and the inevitable letters B.O.

The only furniture in this comfortless room was a *tandour*, the Turkish substitute for a fireplace, being like the *brasero* of the Spaniards, a wooden frame holding a copper vessel full of charcoal, covered by a wadded cloth.

She was dashing her head against the wall and the pillow alternately as she rolled about in pain or delirium; her beautiful silky hair hung all dishevelled over her snowy shoulders, which were quite exposed. Her lips were parched and black, while her face was deadly pale and her eyes unnaturally bright and dilated. Her voice was changed, yet the sound of it thrilled through Cyril to his heart's core. She was raving, and she knew him not.

"God help us—God help us!" moaned Cyril, as he knelt by her side in a passion of tears, and sought caressingly to smooth her tangled tresses and reclose her night-dress which she had rent at the neck.

"Poor young lady," said the soldier's widow, commiseratingly, "she's done a power o' good among our poor fellows! Is she your sister, Captain Wedderburn?"

"No."

And in his agony and answer, the woman seemed instinctively to know all; for after a pause she said—

"Doctor Riversdale says, sir, it's more fever than cholera, and so there might be hopes if—"

"If what? Oh, speak out."

"If her system wasn't so low—but she can't stand the shock. I saw two children of mine die at Varna—die when the blue cholera mist rose like a tide about the tent-pegs, and I saw my poor Tom die here, after his leg were ampertated, and—and," she contiued, bursting into tears, "I knows a look when I sees it in the eye now, and I see it here—so she can't last long, poor thing!"

"How long has she been thus?" asked Cyril, in a choking voice.

"Some hours, sir."

"And before that?"

"She was as calm as a lamb, sir, wishing for a clergyman, and expressing fears that a Captain

Wedderburn—you, I suppose, sir—might visit her, and catch the infection."

And this was his Mary—his plighted wife— she whose nature was so full of those charms which are more attractive than the most brilliant or classic beauty—such winning and pretty ways! Oh how, as he knelt by that wretched bedside, and sought to capture and keep the quick small hand that eluded or repelled him, while her eyes sparkled dangerously—through the mists of the past and horror of the present, memory went back to many a happy, happy day, and to epi- sodes all gone for ever now!

She was raving by turns of her father, of her dead brother Harry, of Cyril himself—and his reproachful heart seemed to bleed as he heard her—of little Mrs. Primer, of the Alderman in London, of the prison, and of a host of persons and places whose names bewildered him; then starting into a sitting position, she pressed her hands on her temples, threw back her hair, and with eyeballs starting from their sockets, uttered a piercing shriek, as she sprang into an imaginary river, and then lay back calm and still, with her arms by her side as the fancied waters closed over her head.

"Please Captain Wedderburn, do leave us for a little, and when she is a little more composed and sensible, I'll fetch you;" and the female nurse half led him out into the Divan Hanée,

which is the central hall of every great Turkish
house, and off which all the other rooms open.
She closed the door—dropped the curtain we
should rather say—and Cyril wearily, and as one
in a nightmare, seated himself on the divan, or
luxurious sofa, which is placed all round this
apartment, and there he remained for a time, like
a man in a dream—but a dream which, with all
its bitterness, did not pass away,

CHAPTER XIV.

THE CITY OF THE SILENT.

WAS it the vision of a distempered brain, he asked of himself, this strange and fantastic Turkish hall (through which the sunlight fell in golden flakes from a double row of upper and lower windows of square form), with all its green and gold arabesques and pious sentences from the koran traced round on scrolls beneath the cornices; was it not like some scene he had witnessed in a theatre, that line of twisted columns and horse-shoe arches dividing the room, beyond which he saw a marble fountain playing, and places like pigeon-holes holding vases and beautiful jars, once filled with cool water, sherbet, or flowers? And could it be possible that Mary Lennox—she whom he used to meet in the old pine thicket, whose cheek had so often reposed on his shoulder by the lonely stile in the glen, was lying there on a wretched straw pallet, amid such strange and foreign surroundings, and at the point of—death! So he sat in a kind of stupor, gazing at a group of the Turkish guard seated drowsily under a sunshade, smoking and listening to the lascivious story of a dervish, whom they would reward with a para or two.

Anon the nurse came, and told him in a whisper that "she was asleep;" and he blessed God for it, in the fervent hope that it might be the forerunner of returning health and strength, and that the crisis might be past. So he went forth to soothe his nerves by a stroll and a cigar, and in about two hours returned to find that Mary had been awake, and that a chaplain of the Duke of Cambridge's division (whom the splinter of a shell had wounded) was with her; that she was quite calm, and preparing and wishing to die.

"But not to leave me!" he exclaimed with sorrowful reproach, and he issued forth again, repassing the Osmanli sentinel, who thought he must be mad to grieve about a woman— "Mashallah! a sick one too!"

In the yard he met Doctor Riversdale, and questioned him; but the old staff surgeon shook his head sorrowfully, and his reply recalled to Cyril the convictions of the nurse.

"There are two expressions in the human face, which when we once see them, Wedderburn, we never forget—the first quick glance of love, and the last long look of death! I have been in love in my day, like most men; and as a soldier have

seen many die on the field and in hospital; and
I have seen death in that girl's face, but blended
with love too!"

" How, Riversdale?"

" When her lips uttered *your* name."

After a time, when he re-entered the Divan
Hanée, the curtain veiling the door was lifted by
the nurse, who beckoned him eagerly, and as he
drew near, the woman, with good taste, withdrew,
while Cyril, in a fresh burst of anguish, threw
himself on his knees by Mary's side, striving, but
in vain, to control his grief.

She stretched out her thin hands towards him,
and gave him a soft, sad smile.

Oh, that glance! that too often furtive glance
which all lovers know, and which is too subtle
for description, has much of power; but it was
not the glance that was now in the weird and
pursuing eyes of Mary,—it was the earnest glance
seen only in the eyes of the dying, but blended
with much of sweetness. So Riversdale was
right.

" I am dying, Cyril," said she, in a low voice.;
" I feel it in my heart."

" You—you, my Mary; oh, it cannot be!" he
whispered with quivering lips and in a passion of
tears.

" Yes, Cyril, my love, I can't last long now."

" Oh! would that my wound had been mortal,
and that I had died before you, darling; we

should then have been re-united, never more to part. But God knows what is best for us."

"And blessed be His holy name, Cyril! Kiss me, darling, while—while I can see you, and can feel my hand in yours. The sun has set very suddenly, surely—on the forehead, darling—on the forehead, not the lip—not the lip!"

"Why, my Mary?"

"There may be death in such a kiss."

"Then welcome be the death!"

"Oh, Cyril!—husband of my heart!" she murmured.

"My plighted wife—my Mary!"

"I am going to my poor papa," she said with childlike simplicity. "He clung, Cyril, to the fragment of his patrimony even as a gallant captain clings to the wreck of his ship, and— and——"

"Yes, Mary; though rash, a true gentleman to the last."

"And he loved me so—my poor papa!"

Then her mind began to wander a little again. Far away from Scutari, from where the hastily buried dead lay on the plain without the walls, —from the wards of the horrid hospital her thoughts went as in a dream,—for so her mutterings showed while her poor head rested on Cyril's neck,—back to Lonewoodlee, to the old grey tower, with its turrets and cape-house of the stormy Border times; to the mossy stile and the thorn trees; to the old Scottish firs, with their red stems, gnarled branches and bronze-like foliage cutting the clear blue sky; to the mountain burn that brawled amid grey rocks and stones, purple heather and golden broom; from the green slopes of the Lammermuirs, to the lonely pastoral hills, where the black-faced wedders browsed and bleated; to places where the scarlet rowan grew, and where the pink and white hawthorn loaded the evening air with fragrance; and in the girl's heart there waxed strong the desire to die—not among her kindred, for kindred had she *none*, but that she might die in her native land, and be laid among the graves where her forefathers lay, in the Lennox-aisle of the old kirk at Willowdean.

But fate had willed it otherwise.

For an hour she lay with her head pillowed on Cyril's heart, and barely conscious of his presence. She was hovering on that Borderland which lies between Time and Eternity—that mysterious frontier from whence the world, and all its interests, must look very small indeed; smaller still its wrongs and its sorrows; dim its doubts, its loves, and allurements.

After a time a shiver, that passed over all the delicate form; a sigh that escaped her; and the fallen jaw, revealing all the pearl-like teeth, announced that all was over!

The light was fading as the sun shed its last

red rays on the Bosphorus, but Cyril lingered long with the dead in his arms; and tenderly, and while his tears fell on them, he kissed her white eyelids after he had closed them for ever, smoothing the long dark lashes on the marble checks; and the widowed nurse, who was hovering without, could not restrain her tears when on peeping in she saw the handsome young officer on his knees, in his blood-stained and tattered uniform, engaged in prayer by the humble pallet whereon the dead girl lay, looking in death purer and lovelier than ever.

*   *   *   *   *

By the hospital regulations all fever patients were buried immediately, to avoid the spread of infection, and so that night saw the last scene of this tragedy.

Four soldiers—wounded Fusileers of Cyril's company, men selected by himself—bore her on their shoulders in a hastily-made coffin to the cemetery without the walls, where lie so many of our dead, the gallant, and in too many instances, perhaps, forgotten victims of the war and pest. The only pall that covered her was a ship's union-jack; it had already served for many in Scutari, and would serve for many more; and Cyril, as he stood at the head of her grave, could see the full round silver moon as it rose up in beauty from the sea of Marmora, throwing far across the plain the shadows of the spectre-like

cypresses that overlook the vast Turkish " City
of the Silent," the seven miles of tombs; and
after the chaplain had concluded the affecting
burial service of the Church of England, not a
sound was heard but the splash of oars in the
Bosphorus, throwing showers of seeming diamonds
upwards, as some light caïque shot to or fro; or
the prolonged howling of some houseless dog, the
ever accursed of the prophet, prowling along the
streets of Scutari.

It was the night of the 20th February; so the
same moon that through a tempest of snow
looked down on the capture of Horace Ramornie
near the Tchernaya, saw his cousin acting in a
very different scene in the great cemetery opposite Seraglio Point.

For a time he sat on a tombstone close by, the
picture of thought and grief, his hands clasped
over the hilt of his sword, which was placed between his knees, and his chin resting on his
hands, his eyes bent on vacancy.

In the last hour or two he seemed to have become older, thinner, greyer, and more stern.

The chaplain kindly gave him his arm, and
his four comrades urged him, in their own plain
fashion, to be comforted, though they could not
comprehend the cause of his grief; but then he
was a favourite officer, and as they put on their
caps and saluted him, ere withdrawing to their
quarters in the convalescent portion of the hos-

pital, they all in unison sympathized with Captain Wedderburn.

And there she lay alone in her grave upon the Asian shore, under the shadow of those giant cypresses, poor Mary Lennox, the last of that ilk of the Lonewoodlee.

After all her miseries, it was a strange and wayward fate!

How bitterly and unavailingly now he repented of his past harshness, suspicions, and injustice to her who was gone—bitterly too, for the time lost by their needless separation; for the false position in which she had so long been placed with his family through mistaken ideas of policy; and he felt in his heart, that surely we suffer our punishments on this earth, and not hereafter.

He had but one embodied thought ever present now—that he had found her in this strange land among Miss Nightingale's good Samaritans; that he had seen the face, again heard the voice of Mary, and held her hand in his; and that never, never more would that beloved face turn to his, and never more her voice fall on his ear!

And she had been true to him, and had loved him to the last! He remembered her warning words of fear and love when he kissed her, and he was not without hope that he might yet die and be laid by her side, for Mary seemed so lonely in her grave; but Cyril Wedderburn was not one of those men who die easily.

Many a solitary hour he lingered by Mary's grave, as if he felt the influence of her presence about him still, and many a fresh chaplet of white roses he hung there; for he could not altogether leave the place where she lay alone—so utterly alone; and times there were when he thought he might have her remains transmitted home and laid beside those of her father at Willowdean. There seemed a soothing yet sorrowful companionship in sitting there and repeating her name to himself, and looking at the turf which covered the grave, and at the little marble cross which marked where she who on her deathbed had called him " the husband of her heart," was lying at peace with God and man.

Poor Cyril! His life was purposeless now, and more than the half of it seemed to have passed away. His thick brown hair came out in handfuls, and he could detect—yet heeded it not now —a grey hair or two in his beard and moustache. All zest for existence, for exertion, for anything, had gone with Mary Lennox; but, nevertheless, idleness soon became intolerable. He speedily reported himself fit for active service, and Riversdale struck him off the sick list. So the tenth of March saw him on board of a steam transport, filled with enthusiastic and cheering convalescents who had partly recovered from their wounds, all anxious to have " another shy at the Ruskies"— all longing to be once more before Sebastopol, where the ceaseless cannon boomed and the bullets went *ping-ping* from the rifle-pits, where the dead lay half buried on the hill slopes, and where in rags and misery the trench guards toiled, —God alone knows for what now: but when steaming up the Bosphorus, the eyes of Cyril were turned to the point of Scutari and to the diminishing outline of the cypresses that overlook "the City of the Silent," for his heart was lying there.

Had Lady Wedderburn known of the catastrophe that imparted such a tone of distraction to the letters of her favourite son, she might have thought, with mingled remorse and satisfaction, that her *wish* would probably be gratified after all.

CHAPTER XV.

In Yaila the days and even the nights were passed by Horace Ramornie in a species of mental torture. The longing for freedom took the form of dreams when darkness fell, and visions haunted him like those of one who suffered from fever. He beheld Gwenny at times encompassed by absurd and fantastic perils, from which he sought in vain to save her. Once she appeared clinging to a fragment of loose rock above a raging sea—the cliffs of the Ernescleugh, or Fast Castle, perhaps—and ere he could aid her—for his limbs felt as if powerless, weak, or fettered—the frail thing to which she seemed to cling gave way and Gwenny disappeared beneath the waves, eliciting a cry from Horace, which brought the Russian guard in wonder to his room.

On other occasions, he wandered in pursuit of her through endless and mysterious galleries, arched passages, and long, long chambers, where, though he could hear her voice, he lost all trace of her in the end, and sought in vain with terror and bewilderment of heart.

But then he had other and more pleasant dreams. He was free! He was again with his company of the Fusileers, in the trenches, among wooden gabions and fascines of straw or sand bags, and the booming of the cannon in Sebastopol came to his ear. He saw the white walls and the green spires of the city rising in the sunshine above the curling smoke of the gun batteries. Then would come the music of the band on the march; again he saw the heights above the Alma glittering with Russian bayonets, and he heard the pleasant voice of Cyril Wedderburn; there was a sound of pistol shots, and then came the pale face and glittering cold eyes of Prince Galitzin; or it might be that he had memories of the mess-room of the corps—the billiard table at Chatham or Canterbury, and he was at pool or pyramid with Bingham or Probyn; and often it was of Willowdean and the days when he came there an orphan from his dead mother's side, and then he saw the stately house with its white peristyle and all its windows glittering in the sun, old Gervase Asloane in his ample waistcoat and black suit hovering about; his aunt, Lady Wedderburn, bowling through the ample lawn in her smart pony phaeton, or Sir John in tweed suit and leather gaiters going with his gun to the preserves, or rambling about, weeder in hand, and

Horace could hear his pleasant voice and see again his bright and benign smile; but only to waken and find himself—a prisoner still in Yaila!

It was after visions such as these, that by the mere force of contrast, his captivity felt intolerable, and equally so, when, after being lost in thought—indulging in some bright daydream, perhaps—he would be roused by the hoarse Russian drums, beaten for parade or some tour of duty, and, starting, would bethink him how, or why he was here in Yaila!

Though the idea of violating his parole of honour, attempting to escape or to quit his prison without being properly exchanged, never occurred to Horace, the manner of Galitzin offensively showed that *he* was suspicious of something of the kind being attempted. Horace was conscious of being watched; that eyes were upon him; and that whenever he went abroad for a solitary ramble, somehow, as if by a singular co-incidence, the two Cossacks, Alexis and Ivan—he never knew, nor cared to know their surnames—were always hovering near. But to have spoken of this would have been unwise, and have excited suspicion.

To a Russian of Tartar descent, subtlety and craft were familiar, even as caprice and tyranny, from the days of his wooden cradle, when he had been taught to thump or kick the image of his patron, Saint Ivan Veliki, and even to thrust it in the fire if he suffered pain from overeating himself with pastillia or other sweetmeats; if he lost his top or marbles, or got cuffed for his insolent petulance by any of his companions. He suspected that few things in this world were ever done for the motives really assigned to them, and he believed that under all that went on, something *else* was going on unseen. So there was a terrible distrust of everyone and everything pervading his whole existence.

He was Muscovite to the heart's core!

One morning Horace was sensible of an unusual commotion in Yaila, after Galitzin's *aide-de-camp*, the Lieutenant of the Princess Maria Paulovna's Hussars, who had been sent to the seashore on some special duty, returned with important tidings for the Prince.

The preceding night had been one of dreadful tempest. The rain had fallen in torrents; and, amid the wild bellowing of the wind, the thunder had been heard, as it rattled in appalling peals over the red marble cliffs of the Tchatr Dagh, and the four copper-covered domes of Yaila.

The drums were beaten, and a certain portion of the garrison got under arms after breakfast. Horace felt a thrill of hope in his heart! Was there about to be an attack—a chance of escape after all, and after those weary, weary months of spring and summer he had endured there?

Day was just breaking, and, in anticipation of

some event, which, if it did not set him free, would at least vary the stupid monotony of his existence, Horace came forth, just as Prince Galitzin, after buckling on his sword, was mounting his horse.

The usual strange and malicious glitter came into his eyes, as he seemed to read the hope of Horace in his eager and excited face; and the latter's emotion seemed to strengthen when he saw the troops bring forth two eighteen-pound guns, and, with their muskets slung, tally on to the drag-ropes, as the field-pieces were without horses.

"By Jove, it did rain and blow last night, Monseigneur le Prince," said Horace, loth to ask any questions, while wishing to invite information. "I have not passed so many sleepless hours since I was in the trenches before Sebastopol, and heard the Lancaster guns pounding away on the right attack."

"And you are longing to be there, again— eh?"

"I cannot deny that I am, indeed."

"You must be patient, Monsieur le Capitaine."

Horace sighed bitterly, and then ventured to say—

"But what is the matter? Have you had an *alerte*, or are you going to be attacked?"

"Nay. 'Tis we who are about to attack!"

"What, or who?"

" I know not whether I should reply, but it is no matter.   Well, an English ship—a yacht, apparently—is reported to be ashore on the rocks, a few miles northward from Alushta; and we are just going to knock her to pieces with those two eighteen-pounders, if the waves do not anticipate us; for Kaminski, my aide-de-camp, reports that there is a heavy sea on, and that she can't last long now."

" A wreck—an unarmed yacht.   To fire on a wreck—is this fair ?"

" *Morbleu !*   Did I not once before say that all things are fair in war and love ? and we are at war just now, I believe. Come on, Tegoborski, we have no time to lose !"

" I dreamed of rats last night, and I thought something would be sure to happen after that, and the wind being so high," grumbled the superstitious old Pulkovnick, as he mounted his horse, while Madame, his wife—in a very becoming *deshabille,* appeared at an open window, where she kissed her large white hand repeatedly to the Prince, who waved his smiling adieux in return.

The hoarse and guttural commands were given, and, at a double-quick, the Infantry—about four hundred in number—left Yaila, dragging the guns and limbers, and having with them several kabitkas, or covered Tartar carts, for plunder, or whatever came ashore.

Some hours elapsed, and Horace felt his heart swelling with indignation.   He pictured, in fancy, the shattered ship, the helpless drowning seamen, and the Russian guns firing round-shot —perhaps grape and cannister—upon them from the heights; just as they did during the dreadful hurricane in the preceding November, when so many of our ships perished along the iron-bound coast of the Black Sea.

Much bitterness was now being imparted to the war on both sides; but chiefly owing to the barbarity of the Russians. Doubtless, there were a few instances of humanity that are worth remembering. Many Russian prisoners who were *paroled* at Lewes, expressed in print, on their return home, their gratitude for the kindness and hospitality they had experienced at English hands; and several of our officers who were prisoners of war in Russia, related the kind treatment they received while there. So, perhaps, Ivan Prince Galitzin was a somewhat exceptional personage.

About noon his cruel expedition returned, and Horace, who had secluded himself in his room, full of disgust and anger, heard the noisy applause with which the soldiers in Yaila received those who came back, though their exploit was far removed from being a noble or gallant one. The kabitkas were filled with pieces of shattered wreck, sheets of copper, sail-cloth, rigging, several cases of wine, London porter, and casks of beef, which had come ashore; and now hearing by chance that prisoners had been taken, Horace,

again came forth to see them, and seek for some
intelligence of the outer world, from which he
was so completely debarred by the measures and
extreme reserve of Galitzin.   To be sure he
might always have gained some news of the war
from Madame Tegoborski, who was not indisposed
to view him with favour, as a handsome young
man ; but he had a wholesome dread of exciting
the jealousy of the Prince in that quarter.

" How many prisoners have you got, Monsieur
le Colonel ?" he asked of Tegoborski, who was
proceeding leisurely, limping, for he was lame,
towards his quarters, anticipating a cup of hot
tea after his morning's work.

" One," was the brief reply ; " at least only
one of any consequence."

" And the rest ?"

" Are in the sea."

" Drowned ?"

" Or shot, as the case may have been."

In the yard of the fortress, Horace perceived
one whom he took to be an Englishman, handcuffed ; he had on only a tattered white shirt and
pair of blue cloth trousers ; he was tall and
athletic in figure, fair complexion, bald and bare-
headed, for in lieu of a cap he had a bloodstained
handkerchief round his head, showing that he had
been wounded ; and he was seated moodily, and
as if lost in thought, on the trail of one of the
fatal eighteen-pounder field-pieces.

He looked up listlessly as Horace approached, and said,

"A prisoner, like myself, I see."

"Not precisely, as I have not the misfortune to be fettered; but I have been here for four months—ever since Sir Colin Campbell's night march to Tchorgoun. And you?"

"My ship went ashore in the middle watch last night, on a reef that is not laid down in any of our charts."

"Where?"

"Within a quarter of a mile of the cliffs that rise near Alushta, a Tartar village on the coast. We had undergone a rough night and were blown far out of course beyond the headland of Alupka, where Prince Woronzoff's castle stands; our rudderbands had given way, and we couldn't help ourselves. Finding that the craft wouldn't last long, I lowered the boat and got the ladies ashore, and at the hazard of my own life returned on board; but I was scarcely on the deck, when, bang, bang, bang from the cliffs came a fire of round shot from these rascally guns; so they and the sea, which was a heavy one, soon made an end of the schooner and of my men, for every poor fellow perished, those who threw themselves into the sea to escape the cannonade being killed by the lances of the Cossack beggars, as they struggled half fainting ashore."

"Most rascally—most base!" exclaimed Horace.

"Luckily I had my naval uniform below, and put it on. As I swam ashore the sight of my epaulettes saved me from being butchered like the rest; but they were torn from my shoulders, and I was handcuffed as you see. I am a lieutenant in Her Britannic Majesty's service! As a signal of distress I had the union-jack reversed at the gaff-peak; but I was glad when the spar was knocked away and it fell into the sea. It went to my heart to see the old bunting under fire and never a shot in return. I thought of Nelson, and the signal that flew along the line at Trafalgar; of old Charlie Napier's in the Baltic, 'Sharpen your cutlasses, lads!' I thought too of many an old shipmate who is lying in the Bight of Benin with a cold shot at his heels, and strong in my breast grew the genuine old English contempt of all these foreign beggars! But now that I look at you again, I think I have had the pleasure of meeting you before. Are you not Captain Ramornie of the Royal Fusileers—the nephew of Sir John Wedderburn of Willowdean?"

"The same; and you?"

"Lieutenant Robert Newnham, R.N."

"And your ship?" asked Horace, faintly.

"Was the Master of Ernescleugh's yacht. I have seen you aboard of her at Cowes more than once."

"And the ladies you spoke of?"

"Were Lady Wedderburn and Lady Ernescleugh ; they *would* come out here after their sons in the Crimea. Lord Cardigan's yacht had come, and the Countess of Errol had accompanied her husband who is in the Rifle Brigade, so the two mammas were determined to come too, and bring no end of comforts and condiments for their 'dear boys' in the trenches ; but by jingo ! they'll rather repent of the expedition now, though they were sent with their maids under escort in a kabitka towards Balaclava ; for the worst of the story is yet to come."

"What could well be worse than that which you have told me ?" exclaimed Horace.

"Another prisoner was brought on with me here, and my heart bleeds for the poor young lady in the hands of those d——d Russians. She is too young for sorrow, and was so kind and affable to all the poor fellows before the mast, they idolized her !"

" Of whom are you talking ?" asked Horace, whose heart began to tremble with apprehension and conjecture.

" Who should I mean but Miss Gwendoleyne Wedderburn ?"

" She here ?"

"Aye, here in this fortress of Yaila—a prisoner like ourselves—but not half so safe in some respects."

" My God !" exclaimed Horace, and he shivered from head to foot; " how came it to pass, Newnham, that she was not also sent to Balaclava?"

"In this fashion, for I was standing by, and to my sorrow and disgust heard every word.

"'I am rich, Monseigneur le Prince,' said Lady Wedderburn, in the greatest agitation, to the Russian commander, whom I understood to be a Prince Galitzin—but that's a name like Smith in England, they are thick as Mother Cary's chickens in Russia; 'and so is my friend; we can afford to pay a ransom, if it will be taken.'

"'And your niece, or daughter, which is the young lady?' he asked.

"'My niece — Mademoiselle Gwendoleyne Wedderburn.'

"'Wedderburn, Wedderburn,' repeated the Russian, 'she is wealthy too; an Indian heiress, I understood.'

"'Yes, Monseigneur; but how knew ou that?'

"'A Monsieur Chesters told me all about it at Balaclava; and of her being the intended of your son; who was wounded or killed at the Alma, I believe.'

"'Only wounded, thank Heaven! but do you know Monsieur le Capitaine Chesters?'

"'I *did* know him; but, Madame, he is dead and buried now,' replied the other, with a grin.

" 'And now about a ransom?' said Lady Wedderburn, full of anxiety.

" 'Well, Madame, no ransom can be taken for the young Hospoza; we are Russian troops, not Circassians, Bedouin robbers, or brigands.'

" 'But her liberty?' urged Lady Wedderburn, to whom Miss Gwenny clung in terror and despair.

" 'Her liberty shall be well cared for. I shall keep her for myself; heiresses are scarce in the Crimea,' was the bantering reply.

" 'Surely you will permit me to accompany her?' urged poor Lady Wedderburn, piteously.

" 'What the deuce should we do with old women in Yaila? It would only be people to feed unprofitably, and in this nothing-for-nothing world, my dear Madame——'

" 'Oh, dearest aunt, are we to be separated?' exclaimed Miss Gwenny, in dreadful agitation.

" 'Instantly, by St. Ivan Veliki!'

" The wretches tore them asunder, though the aunt and niece clung to each other with the death-like clutch of the drowning, and their cries wrung my heart. The two elder ladies were sent in a Tartar waggon towards Balaclava, in charge of the aide-de-camp Kaminski and four Cossacks, one of whom carried a white handkerchief as a flag of truce on the point of his lance, while we were brought on here. But Heaven help the poor girl, Captain Ramornie. Galitzin

sees that she is young and beautiful, and he
knows that she is wealthy, for I heard him remark, laughingly, to Kaminski, his aide, 'This
war can't last for ever; another winter will see
those allies frozen or fought out; then I shall go
to England with my wife, turn her rupees into
roubles, and spend them in Holy Russia.'   Holy
Russia be d—d, say I !"

Horace listened to all this with the air of one
quite stunned by a calamity; and he was again
about to address Newnham, when the voice of
Galitzin was heard.

" No talking—no communications between
you two.   Separate them," he added to the
parvoschick of the main guard; "and as the
sailor has declined to give his parole, keep him
a close prisoner."

So poor Newnham was led away.

" I was only hearing some details of the—
well, I suppose we must call it the shipwreck,"
said Horace, making a prodigious effort to appear
calm and to conceal the agony of his spirit; for
the idea of Gwenny being a prisoner in Yaila
seemed too fantastic, too unexpected, and too
horrible for conviction.

" Ah ! we let him put the women ashore; for
whatever you may think, we are not quite devoid
of gallantry, we Russians; and then we knocked
the schooner to pieces," said Galitzin, laughing;
" but the chief prize we brought on here."

" I do not understand you," faltered Horace.

" Then understand this. I have caught the rich cousin—the brunette—the little Anglo-Indian millionaire, whose intended I pistolled at the Alma——"

" Cyril Wedderburn ?"

" Well, yes, if that *was* his name; I suppose we may speak of him in the past tense now."

" From whom had *you* all this private information ?"

" From Monsieur Chesters, *le scelerat !*"

" When ?"

" When I met him in the camp of the Turkish Contingent."

" Explain, Monseigneur le Prince ?"

" A few days before your silly night march to Tchorgoun, and when I was figuring, as the play-bills say, ' positively for the last time,' as a Captain of Zouaves," replied the unabashed Russian.

" Will not the offer of a bribe set her free ?"

" Not twenty bribes !"

" Why, Monseigneur le Prince ?"

" You shall hear in good time."

" And where is she now ?" asked Horace, with an affectation of carelessness that certainly cost him an effort.

" In the apartments and under the matronage of Madame Tegoborski. She was dreadfully offended when I attempted to give her a little salute *à la Russe*. St. Ivan Veliki—bah! a time shall come when she will think little of my wiry moustache—though it *is* like a hog's-bristle— being rasped on her damask cheek!"

"By Jove! this *is* a pleasant situation," thought Horace, as he wiped his brow, and longed to plant his foot upon the neck of Major-General Prince Galitzin, who added with pleasing condescension—

"I shall introduce you to her at old Tego-borski's to-night; but perhaps you don't care about it."

"Thanks, Monseigneur le Prince, I shall come with pleasure," said Horace; and he retired to his room with a heart that was full, nigh to bursting, with sorrow, terror of the present, and apprehension of the future.

That night Newnham was dispatched on foot, escorted by two Cossack Lancers, towards Yekaterinoslav, and a deadly fear came over Horace that unless he dissembled, and he and Gwenny played "their cards" remarkably well, some such distant transmission might await himself, if Galitzin discovered the deep and tender interest they had in each other.

And how to conceal it? for the first meeting might, most perilously, reveal all!

"Gwenny here—my Gwenny here in Yaila?" he repeated to himself again and again.

He felt himself trembling from head to foot;

a pallor came over him repeatedly, as the blood rushed back upon his heart. Though loving her with all the devotion of which his life and heart were capable, he had no desire, even while longing passionately to see her, to have her with him there, and his voice shook while, clasping his hands, he said fervently—

"God protect her—my darling Gwenny. Oh! I fear she will need all His protection here in Yaila!"

CHAPTER XVI.

TEA WITH MADAME TEGOBORSKI.

HORACE naturally wondered how it came to pass that Chesters should have spoken of the Wedderburn family or of their private interests to an utter stranger—a foreigner—a mere chance visitor, such as this pretended Captain of Zouaves in the redoubts before Balaclava; for the visit of Galitzin had been paid to them prior to the assault made by the Russians on the day of the battle there; but it only proved that the enmity of Chesters to Cyril was an ever-rankling subject, and the matter might have come about *apropos* of the misfortune which befel the latter at the Alma. And then the luckless Major of the Turkish Contingent had failed as yet to recognise in the turbaned Zouave his quondam gambling acquaintance; but the latter knew *him* only too well, and treasured up his secret vengeance. However the matter came to pass, Horace was certain of one thing, that the information of the needy Russian Prince as to Gwenny's fortune was unpleasantly accurate.

His next idea was, as to how he and she were to meet, and how to greet each other—betrothed lovers, who had been so long and so perilously parted—in the presence of Galitzin, after the openly-expressed views of that personage concerning her—views so suddenly and distinctly stated. For Horace knew that the Prince had nothing in the world but his sword, his epaulettes, and a truly Muscovite spirit for the most daring peculation; and he knew also how resolute, how cunning, and how savage he could be when roused.

And now, by the contingencies of war, this man was to become the arbiter of their destinies!

Longing, with all a young lover's ardour, to fold Gwenny in his arms, and to cover her sweet face and hands with kisses, he would, nevertheless, be compelled to appear before her as a stranger, and, as such, to be introduced by the Russian ogre, who had them both in his power.

It seemed intolerable and absurd, and times there were when Horace was on the point of saying boldly that the lady was his betrothed, his intended, and almost a kinswoman; but then prudence suggested that such a confidence might be unwise, and might, moreover, cause Galitzin to dispatch him, under escort, to Yekaterinoslav, if he did not *dispatch* him out of the world altogether. For Horace could not forget the fate of Ralph Chesters, and knew the refined cruelty of which the Prince was capable.

Gwenny, ere evening came, had got over much of her terror of the shipwreck; but her mind was still brooding with horror over the memory of the cannonade, the mangled and drowning seamen, and the strange manner in which she had been so rudely separated from her aunt and Lady Ernescleugh, and brought she knew not whither. But the Prince had pacified her for a time, by the assurance that when he could get a carriage worthy of conveying her, she should be also sent to Balaclava.

She was full of these things, and in no mood to construe, or attempt to understand Madame Tegoborski, who, as she could not speak English, addressed her in Russian, mingled with a few words of German, seeking to interest her in a certain handsome young "Capitaine Ramhornoff," whom she was soon to see, and whom Gwenny supposed to be some odious Russian, who ate tallow candles and took his morning libation of train oil.

Horace felt the absolute necessity of losing no time in letting her know the line of conduct they must adopt towards each other, lest she should become inspired by doubt or apprehension of his seeming coldness.

On the flyleaf of a Russian book he pencilled a few words in the smallest possible space, simply informing her that under the eyes which were on them there, they must seem to be only *friends*, not what they really were; and that, on the first opportunity, he should explain all; and he had barely achieved this tiny billet, when Galitzin appeared to inquire " If he was ready to accompany him and his aide-de-camp, the Lieutenant Kaminski ?"

The Prince was in full uniform, with a pair of splendid epaulettes set very high upon his shoulders in the Russian fashion. He was evidently bent on making an impression, for he wore a gold embroidered waistbelt, and in addition to the order of St. Anne, had that of St. Andrew, an order founded by Peter the Great in 1699, and only bestowed on officers of high military degree. It was a blue enamelled saltire with the Muscovite eagle, and four initials, signifying *Sanctus Andreas, Patronus Russiæ.* Horace had only the poor remains of his red coat, on which none of the lace and few of the buttons remained; but he knew that to Gwenny's eye " the old red rag that tells of England's glory" would be dearer and more significant than the most splendid costume in the world. However, he felt that he cut but a sorry figure in comparison with Galitzin.

He was greatly agitated on entering the whitewashed vaulted chamber, which, in one of the old towers, passed as the drawing-room of

Madame Tegoborski; but though the latter was there, and received Horace with a bland smile, and the Prince with a particularly bright one, Gwenny had not yet left her room, so the visitor glanced uneasily about him, after shaking the hand of the grim Pulkovnick, or *Chef de Bataillon*.

Most of the furniture in the apartment seemed strange to the eye, and extremely nautical in fashion; for save a piano, taken *sans cérémonie* from the house of an Armenian merchant at Alushta, most of it was the spoil of that hurricane in the Black Sea which strewed the shore with wrecks in the preceding November. Wafered on the wall were two Russian caricatures, which at that time were thought prime jokes. One represented John Bull in his well-known top boots, occupying an island so small that he had not room to turn in it, and which was divided into three parts, entitled "Leinster, Oxford, Cambridge." The other was a grotesque figure of Sir Charles Napier, presenting a fish from the Baltic Sea to the British Parliament, as the spoil of Cronstadt and Bomarsund.

An *eikon* or Byzantine Madonna stood in a corner, with metal halo like a gilt horseshoe around the head; but now there was a muslin veil drawn discreetly over it, lest it should see old Tegoborski become tipsy, or the Prince saluting Madame, which, we must admit, he was wont to do somewhat oftener than friendship warranted, or platonic affection required.

Madame Norina Paulovna Tegoborski, a stout and very fair woman, with a dazzling neck and bosom, was beautifully dressed in honour of the evening, and wore Schologoleff earrings, each like four tiny cannon-balls, a fashion adopted in honour of an imaginary artillery officer, who with only *four* guns, was alleged by the Russians to have sorely mauled and repulsed the allied fleets at Odessa !   On her large, fair arms were glittering bracelets ; but on this occasion she was fated to display her charms in vain.

The room door opened, there was the rustling of a dress, and Horace felt a mist before his eyes and a wild throbbing in his heart, as Gwenny, looking pale and startled, yet somewhat defiant in bearing, entered.   The Prince hurried to kiss her hand, and next Madame Tegoborski hastened to present to her the Aide-de-camp Kaminski, and " le Capitaine Ramhornoff."

" Horace !" exclaimed the poor girl in utter bewilderment, " you *here* ?"

" And you, Gwenny ?"   He clasped her hands, and—had death menaced them both, to resist the impulse was impossible — for a moment their flushed faces were pressed together, but the hands remained closely locked, while her agitation found relief in a flood of tears.

" The Prince has told me all," said Horace,

" and more than I could wish to have heard."

" I certainly expected to see you in the Crimea —and dear Cyril too," said Gwenny, sobbing.

" Alas ! I know nothing of him ; I have been here for more than four months."

"We heard that he had left Scutari and joined the Fusileers again."

" Recovered ?"

" Yes."

" Thank Heaven—poor Cyril."

" What is all this?—you are old friends, I find!" said the Prince, as Horace drew back (after contriving to slip his billet into the hand of Gwenny and to whisper, " Read at leisure"). " But, I suppose," he added, laughing, and point-ing to one of the caricatures, " all the people in your little island know one another, it is so small."

For a traveller writes : " The notion that the great want of England is want of land, is a very popular one in Russia, where land is so plentiful in proportion to the population that no proprietor thinks of reckoning his fortune by his acres, but by the number of peasants he can put to culti-vate them."

And now Horace and Gwenny sat on opposite sides of the room, their eyes and hearts full of each other; but all external emotion was repressed by the consciousness of publicity—the odious presence of strangers.

"And you were taken prisoner, my poor Horace?" said Gwenny, in a tender tone.

"Yes. In the dark amid the snow I fell into the hands of the enemy, in the night expedition to Tchorgoun."

"And hence the mystery of your disappearance and the total cessation of all letters. You know, of course, the catastrophe of last night and this morning?"

"I have heard all from poor Newnham and the Prince," replied Horace, in a sad voice.

Gwenny looked at him earnestly.

She could see that captivity, irritation, and the suspicions of Galitzin had done no good to Horace. His eyes, she thought, had lost much of their open, candid, and kind expression; they seemed sunken, furtive, and at times defiant and stern. He looked more manly, however, for campaigning and trench work had developed and hardened his frame; but he was bearded to the eyes, and tattered as a digger at Ballarat.

The figure of Gwenny, he thought, had attained more of the roundness of womanhood; her face was pale and pure as ever, her smile as winning, and her bearing as full of grace.

"Horace—Horace!" she exclaimed, with a touch of her old waggery, "such a coat you have—why, it is in absolute rags!"

"Yes, Gwenny; my kit is not at its best—or my wardrobe, I should have to say, were Aunt

Wedderburn here; but the Cossacks took a fancy
for the lace and most of the buttons; they appre-
ciate finery, those fellows.   But your own attire
is rather odd.   That dress never came from Swan
and Edgar's!"

"It is a yellow silk of Madame Tegoborski's—
as you see, a world too wide for me."

Galitzin, who was equally master of English as
of French, laughed at these remarks.   But now
the *samovar*, or brass urn, made its appearance,
hissing and hot, and the important business of the
evening, tea drinking, commenced.

The four Russians all turned to the *eikon* and
crossed themselves, while a servant poured out
the tea, and another—a pretty Karaïte Jewess,
whose white *fereedjè* gave additional lustre to her
beautiful eyes—handed it round, with cakes and
preserved fruit. It was served in crystal tumblers*
for the four gentlemen, but in china cups for the
two ladies; and the imbibing of this fluid is such
a passion with the Russians, that in the *Traktirs*,
or tea-houses, of Moscow and St. Petersburg,
visitors have been known to take from twelve to
twenty cups at a sitting.

Gwenny made more than one wry face over
her cup, for in lieu of cream, a slice of lemon was
floating in it.   Old Pulkovnick Tegoborski added

---

* The use of the tumbler is being gradually banished.—
" The Russians at Home."

to his tumbler a good jorum of rum, and after having it filled five or six times, hobbled into a corner, where he proceeded to intrench himself behind the columns of the *Moskauer Zeitung*, and was soon enveloped in a cloud from his meerschaum. The Prince sat by the side of Gwenny and sought to draw all her attention to himself, while Madame Tegoborski looked at them vindictively over her tea equipage.

We have mentioned that the Pulkovnick was lame, and we may add that he became so in a very remarkable manner. He was the aide-de-camp whose foot—as M. de Custine relates—the Emperor Nicholas pinned to the floor with the point of his sword, to convince a distinguished foreigner how perfect was the submission of his officers !

A serf by birth, he had attained to the fifth *tchinn,* or grade · of nobility, with his colonel's commission, through the *oukase* issued by Nicholas in 1842, when serfs were first permitted to make civil contracts and to hold property.

CHAPTER XVII.

GALITZIN AS A LOVER.

GALITZIN was well educated and knew all the little that existed then of Russian literature; thus he made many an excuse of translating to Gwenny the tender passages which he had marked off in the poems of the Countess Rostopchin (which being secret literature, circulate in *MS.* only) or the verses of Puschkin, who has sung so sweetly of the Fountain of Tears in the palace of the Crimean Khans, or in the story of Voina-roffski, the lover of Aurora of Konigsmark; but she listened vacantly or with ill-disguised impatience, and would irritate him by ever and anon addressing Ramornie.

"And so, dear Horace, you are a captain now?" said she, in the middle of one of Voina-roffski's most passionate appeals.

"Yes, Gwenny; but I got my promotion through the death of the very man who would have been the first to congratulate me on it—yes; to have ordered a fresh cooper of port at

the mess to wet the new commission—poor Jack
Probyn! But it was no fault of mine; it was
the fortune of war; yet I would rather have remained a lieutenant still, and had jolly Jack to
make fun with."

"We shall have peace soon, Mademoiselle,"
said the Prince, adding the same in Russian to
Madame Tegoborski; and Horace shivered, for
he knew what idea was associated in the mind of
Galitzin with peace.

"But peace always ends in war," said Madame
Tegoborski, "just as war must end in peace.
What you say reminds me of a passage in Kriloff, the Fabulist, about the friendship of two
dogs."

"And what says your Kriloff?" asked Galitzin, knitting his brow.

"It is a fable only."

"Well, go on with your fable."

"Two dogs in a court-yard become affectionate
friends; how they fawn and love each other, and
will never fight again. It is charming; but
suddenly a bone is thrown from a window, and
they straightway proceed to tear each other to
pieces."

"Yes; and Kriloff has another fable of a
sleeping peasant, who is about to be stung by a
serpent; but a friendly fly bites him on the nose
and awakes him. The shepherd kills the serpent,
but he also destroys the fly. A warning to the

meddlesome, or the jealous, not to be too officious in *opening the eyes* of any one," added Galitzin with considerable significance of meaning, after which Madame coloured, lapsed again into silence and took a cigarette, but she had to twist it up for herself that evening.

Monseigneur le Prince was otherwise occupied, he forgot all about the little duty which had been a pleasure yesterday; and now desiring Kaminski to open the piano, he begged Gwenny to favour them with a little music.

With a horrid memory of the events of the morning hovering in her mind Gwenny was about to decline, when a. glance from Horace decided her, and she seated herself at the instrument — a very indifferent one, and not at all improved in its recent transmission from Alushta, by Cossacks, on the limber of a brass field-piece.

All the music placed before her was Russian, but Gwenny's fingers and ears were clever, and after a few efforts she was able to read off and play in very tolerable style—" *The Red Sarafan*," (so called from the old Muscovite dress worn by ladies at evening parties), Vielgorski's *Buivala*, and even the " Nightingale," a traditional song and air of the Russian gipsies, to the great enchantment of Galitzin, who was flattering himself what a creditable little wife she would be; and even of old Tegoborski, whose grizzled and closely shorn caput and grim visage (seamed by the edge of more than one Osmanli sabre), appeared approvingly above the columns of the *Zeitung*, as he waved his meerschaum and beat time with his lame foot; but more than all were they pleased when her rapid little fingers dashed over in quick succession all the melodies of the inevitable and inimitable *Trovatore.*

And Horace listened like one in a dream. Was it reality, or was it a madness that had come upon him, that he seemed to be sitting in Crimean Yaila, and under the shadow of the Tchatr Dagh, listening to Gwenny Wedderburn playing the self-same airs which she had played to him in the early days of their loverhood, and on many a delicious and half-dreamy evening in the beautiful drawing-room at Willowdean.

"I have been tired of my own company," said he in a low voice, as he bent over her, "and have longed —with all the longing of a desperate and a loving heart—to be beside you again, but *not* here. Oh, no, not here; in my wildest imaginings, no such idea or wish could have occurred to me, and yet it has come to pass. Oh! what madness tempted Lady Wedderburn and Lady Ernescleugh to venture here?"

" To see their sons. Besides, Lord Cardigan's yacht, and ever so many more, have come out. And you mentioned having seen the Countess of Errol with her husband in the camp of the Rifles."

"True; but what of that? This barbarous land is no place for delicate English ladies; and I would to heaven that I saw you safe on the watery high road for home."

Much more they rashly succeeded in whispering to each other, for Galitzin was at that moment in conference with Kaminski. How tender and delicious to themselves—but themselves only—are the little nothings that make up the conversation of lovers!

Was it Ennemoser's theory of polarity, or what? But it seemed that in the same mysterious fashion as that on which the learned doctor expatiates, through spirituality, or may it be the force of a strong love, a kind of magnetic current had passed between these two at times, for on comparison they found that they had simultaneously thought of, or dreamt each of the other, and imagined the same things at the same identical moment.

It might be all nonsense, or a mistake; but anyway it was a delicious theme to talk about, till the eyes of Galitzin were upon them, and he had begun to feel first piqued, and then jealous of Horace as an *Anglais;* but luckily, he was equally so of the aide-de-camp Kaminski, who having discovered a pair of glazed boots and some kid gloves in a chest that came ashore from the shattered yacht—some of poor Newnham's holiday finery, perhaps—had appeared in them as for special service this evening.

Giving the obsequious Kaminski a hint to draw off Horace and engage him in conversation, Galitzin bent over Gwenny's chair.

"Ah, Mademoiselle, your singing enchants me; that *Miserere* was indeed divine!" he whispered, in what he deemed his most seductive tone, as he proceeded to turn over the leaves really like a well-bred man of the world rather than the savage he was in heart. "But," he added, as the cruel glitter came into his dark eyes, "excuse me—I have begun to dislike your friend."

"Who?" asked Gwenny, impetuously.

"He in the tattered red coat."

"What—poor Horace?" she exclaimed, and then blushed with confusion and irritation.

"Orace—what you mean the Hospodeen Ramhornoff?"

"He is indeed an old *friend*," replied Gwenny, in alarm, for ere this she had read the pencilled note, and could think of no safer term for him.

"Bah! I hate such old, or rather such young friends." Then after a pause, he added with a loftiness that made her smile, "I am the Prince Galitzin, Major-General under the Emperor, Knight of the Imperial Orders, and Colonel of the Tambrov Regiment of Infantry.

She only gave an acquiescent bow; had he been that worthy grocer and self-righteous elder of the kirk who officiated as Baron-Bailie of Willowdean, she could not have seemed less awed.

Now Galitzin knew enough of the world, of

Europe, of that isle of it named Britain, and of the
" snobbery " thereof, to believe that she would be
greatly impressed by his announcement, as well
as by his stars, medals, and enormous epaulettes ;
but she had come from a land where Rajahs,
Maharajahs, Begums, Nanas, and Princes were
thick as leaves in Vallombrosa, and where she
had seen them trotting about on white elephants
with all their half-naked *suwarri* yelling at their
heels, so she " saw nothing in it."

But as the evening wore on, an eventful one in
the life of her and Horace, Madame Tegoborski
strove, but in vain, to open a flirtation first with
him and then, as he was too *triste,* with the
staff-officer, Kaminski, and to turn the tables on
the heedless Prince. The latter was, however,
too fully occupied with Gwenny to perceive this,
or to care one jot about it ; and certainly, the
grim old Pulkovnick, Alexis Tegoborski, appeared to care quite as little ; he seemed entirely occupied with the pot-hooks and endless
lines of consonants which seemed to make up
the letter-press of the *Moskauer Zeitung ;* and
for the remainder of the evening, Horace discreetly kept apart from Gwenny.

With the views of Galitzin so openly stated
and now attempted to be put in force, they felt
that to observe a distant reserve to each other
was absolutely necessary ; for if the gallant commander of the Tambrov Infantry had suspected

that his prisoner was a secret—and still more, an accepted—lover, he would have no more compunction for telling off a file of Cossacks to take him into the nearest wood, and there despatch him with their carbines, than for taking an extra glass of kinmel, or spoonful of caviare before saying his prayer at dinner time.

However, after that evening Horace was invited no more to tea-drinkings or other entertainments at the apartments of Madame Tegoborski; not that the latter was to blame there, for the wishes of the Prince came to her through her husband, and they were law, for the Russian wife must not forget the symbolical whip which her husband receives from her father on the bridal day.

Long, long were the watches of the night in which he thought, and thought, and considered of what was to be done, till it seemed as if his brain would turn. Then came sleep, full of nervous starts and dreams, and then came the morning.

It was a horror to wake with the first thought that rushed upon him, like a black and overwhelming flood, the knowledge that by an extraordinary turn in the wheel of fortune—a cast of evil destiny—Gwendoleyne Wedderburn was in Yaila, at the mercy of that lawless Russian officer, and in the care, custody and apartments, of one whom he had too much reason to deem alike unscrupulous and jealously hateful of her—Madame Tegoborski.

Of what vengeance might not such a woman be capable!

And if Gwenny, a helpless being, a stranger and prisoner of war, escaped the bold designs of the Prince, might she not, by poison perhaps, fall a victim to the vengeance of the forgotten mistress!

Galignani and the *Times* record such vengeances every day. So what might not occur in the sequestered fort of Yaila?

CHAPTER XVIII.

THE PROGRESS HE MADE.

LITTLE knowing the peculiarity of the perils that surrounded her, Gwenny felt tolerably secure in Yaila, chiefly because Horace Ramornie was there, and only once or twice did she reflect on how strange and horrible her isolation and detention would have been had he *not* been there by being a prisoner elsewhere, or with the army before Sebastopol. But Gwenny did not like gloomy thoughts, so she speedily thrust these aside.

When safe at home and free it would be something great to talk about, to remember, and to think of—it would be like a leaf from a romance, the fact that they should have *both*, he and she, been together prisoners of war in a Russian fortress. And then the revelation of their engagement (that terrible secret) must eventually come about pleasantly, even to Aunt Wedderburn; as for good, easy Sir John, Gwenny stood in no awe of him.

She complained to Madame Tegoborski that she saw but little of Captain Ramornie, for repeatedly when he had called at the quarters of the Pulkovnick, the Karaïte maiden in the white fereedji, made incomprehensible excuses for not admitting him. Horace knew well why this came about; but Madame, who only half understood the queries of her guest, could only shrug her shoulders and make grimaces in reply. Galitzin, however, stated to her, that it was deemed improper to permit frequent conferences between those who were prisoners in a fortress, on the principle of military expedience.

This explanation, though utter nonsense, partially satisfied the girl for a time, and she could only sigh and watch incessantly at the window in the hope of seeing Horace pass through the yard before the barracks.

So never dreaming that danger menaced her, she sometimes took merry bursts of laughter at the abrupt and inflated love-making of Galitzin which he sometimes conducted in French as well as English; but her untimely merriment caused his dark eyes to gleam and his brow to become purple with passion, while bitter and evil thoughts of violence flashed upon his lawless mind.

But Gwenny, though she knew it not, had one great safety in the fact that the love of Galitzin was almost destitute of all passion; and provided that he obtained her hand and fortune by an undoubtedly legal marriage, which not even the law of England could break, he cared for little else. Yet it *was* pleasing to him, the conviction that the girl so completely in his power and at the mercy of his passions, was one possessed of beauty, accomplishments, and vivacity.

And poor Horace as he walked about in the gravelled yard or square, under the irritating observation of a long grey-coated Russian sentinel, chafed when he heard Gwenny's voice through the open window as she sang and played in the drawing-room of Madame Tegoborski, for the delectation of Galitzin ; and also on other occasions, when he saw the latter mounted to accompany her and her " matron " for a drive in the Tartar pony-carriage of the latter to the village of Alushta, Babugan Yaila, or to Bagtche Serai, from the high road to which the valley of Inkerman, with its perforated cliffs and ruined fortress was visible, with an old Genoese bridge in the foreground ; and in the distance, by the aid of a telescope, they could from thence see the green domes of Sebastopol and the white tents of the right flank of the British camp, at which Gwenny would cast many a wistful glance. Ramornie always viewed their departure on these expeditions with something of terror, lest they might not *return,* for he knew not what nefarious plans might be forming in the inscrutable mind of Galitzin, and his best hope lay in the chance of their falling in with and being carried off by some foraging or scouting party of the allied cavalry.

But on one evening after their return from a drive, and when Madame Tegoborski had gone on some mission to a Russian church among the mountains close by, Galitzin found himself alone with Gwenny and hastened to improve the opportunity; for the old Pulkovnick, shrewdly conceiving himself to be in the way, had taken his forage cap and meerschaum and limped forth to enjoy the latter on the gun-battery which faced the road to the Tchatr Dagh.

"What say you, Mademoiselle," he whispered with a soft smile during a pause in her playing; "how should you like to become a Princess?"

"I know not—I never thought of such a thing."

"The dignity would well become your beauty, and you could then be the mistress of peasants who should be to you as slaves—people whose teeth you might even draw, if you could find among them one white enough to replace a lost one of your own."

"A most shocking idea! I never saw a princess; but in India I have seen a Begum riding on a snow-white elephant, in a golden howdah, hung with scarlet silk."

"I could not exactly give you all that," said the Prince (and indeed he might have added, "nor anything else;") "but I can assure you that there is no nobler title in Russia than that of Galitzin."

" Oh, I perceive ; you are pleading for yourself !" said Gwenny, laughing, amid her well-acted surprise.

" Do you not understand the spirit of all I have said to you ?" he asked, gravely.

" I think so."

" How then, this laughter ?" he asked.

" We are here in a horrid old prison, apparently, as in a dull house in the country," said Gwenny, still endeavouring to parry his addresses. " You have paid me certain well-bred attentions, such as every pretty girl expects. You praise my singing, which I know to be tolerable—my playing too, which I know to be good ; and you seem to like my society, which I am vain enough to conceive must be much more pleasant than that of old Tegoborski, or of Madame his wife, but all this must end."

" How so, and when ?"

" I shall soon be released ; I am a non-combatant," said she, smiling ; " to detain me is simply absurd, and I have powerful friends who will not forget me."

" St. Ivan Veliki ! we shall see what we *shall* see !" said he, through his set teeth.

And Gwenny laughed again with her head waggishly on one side, as she ran her fingers over the ivory keys of the piano.

She knew not what Horace did; that she was in the hands of a dissipated and *blasé* wretch, a world-weary reprobate, who had long since done with all human emotions, save avarice, and perhaps a little of lust. He was artful, however, and thought to enlist her vanity in his favour.

"Your life must be dull here?" he resumed.

"Very," said she, sighing.

"I could soon remove you to the wonders of St. Petersburg."

"Thank you—but dull as it is, I should prefer remaining here."

"Why?" asked he, with surprise.

"I am nearer the British before Sebastopol."

"I don't think that will matter much to you now," said he, with a wicked glitter in his eyes; but the expression was unseen by Gwenny, for during this conversation she never turned her face towards him.

"As the wife of a Galitzin you will be equal in rank with the Dolgourukis, the Volhonskis, and the noblest in Russia—even with those who boast of their descent from Rurik of Kiev."

All this did not convey much to Gwenny's ear.

"I am utterly sick of this place and of old Tegoborski; a married officer is never a good boon companion or a jolly comrade. He becomes a man with selfish interests. Ah, if his wife were only like you!"

Gwenny did not understand this wish; but it conveyed a volume. He then proceeded to expatiate on the gaieties to which he pretended he could introduce her, and on the post he could get her in the household of the Empress; on the charms of the opera house at St. Petersburg, where she might hear the national hymn and grand military chorus composed by Lvcoff, who in the latter had always at his disposal forty-eight pieces of artillery, which are discharged by him with the aid of a galvanic wire; he next dwelt on the splendour of the palace of the Czars, with its Granovataya Palata, or reception-room; of the hall of St. George with its alabaster walls; of that of St. Andrew, which seems to have been carved out of rose-coloured marble; of the brilliant entertainments, the promenades à la Polonaise, the balls and banquets to which he should introduce her; but Gwenny only smiled wearily, and relinquishing the piano, proceeded to fan herself.

"Think too, Mademoiselle, of the grand field days in the presence of the august Emperor, when you shall see a glittering array of perhaps three hundred thousand men, of all the races composing mighty Russia, the infantry of Muscovy and Poland, the horsemen of the Don and the Dnieper, and from the steppes of Circassia, defiling past the grand stand, where you sit among the ladies of the Imperial Court. Oh, what is all the army of your little island, when

compared to a show like that? Then there are
masked balls at the Kremlin in Moscow; ah,
you must see that Kremlin," he added, with
something of true enthusiasm, " at the hour of
vespers, when, as Mouravieff says, ' to the call of
the golden headed giant, Ivan Veliki, suddenly
respond from all sides those bells, the voices of
his numberless children, and the sound reverbe-
rates through the startled air—the many, silver-
voiced sound, formed not out of the tolling alone,
but out of thoughts, feelings and words which
fall not to the earth.' "

And thus translating rapidly from memory,
Galitzin spoke all this as if he actually felt it;
but Gwenny only muttered " barbarians," under
her breath, however, and fanned herself more
vigorously than ever; while Galitzin—who in
reality was tabooed by his sovereign, and had
not the power to have introduced her anywhere,
though he sketched so freely castles in the air
out of her own fortune—as he looked down on
the dazzling whiteness of her slender throat, and
the little delicate ears, at each of which a simple
jet-drop dangled, thought to himself, " how
could I ever, for an instant, have admired the
amplitude of Norina Paulovna, with her Schologoleff cannon balls, and large fat fingers covered
with rings?"

" I shall even try to get you an elephant to

ride upon," he resumed. "I suppose you rode one in India?"

Amid her vexations, and they were not small, Gwenny could not help laughing at this offer; and Galitzin, finding her still in the mood to ridicule him, twisted up his moustachios angrily and left her with a haughty bow.

Her child-like entreaties that she might be permitted to write to her aunt, only excited the genuine merriment of the Prince; but Horace was not without hope that the wretched exploit of pounding the stranded yacht with cannon shot, and the sudden appearance of the two ladies at Balaclava, might have the effect of getting an expedition dispatched, for the purpose of capturing and destroying the somewhat paltry fortress of Yaila.

From thenceforward, all the conversations of Galitzin with Gwenny tended towards St. Petersburg and Moscow the holy. The officers and troops in the Crimea were daily being changed, and he would get his command transferred from thence to one or other of those cities; and she devoutly hoped he might be successful.

He saw that the hackneyed, "the venerable protestations which lovers from time immemorial have uttered," were useless with her; yet he felt himself compelled to recur to them.

Once, when he held her hand almost forcibly

and kissed it, she said to him with quiet energy, " I entreat you to respect me, and be kind to me here, in my unfortunate position, as if I were your younger sister, or your daughter."

" My sister, perhaps," replied Galitzin, making a grimace, as the alternative suggested an unpleasant disparity of years; " I have seen much of life in all its phases; I have felt much, suffered much, and enjoyed much; but never knew till now that a passing glance, a smile, could be so priceless to me—never till I met you. Ah, there are higher prizes in this world than courtly rank or military glory; and how often need I reiterate that I love you! You must marry me, Mademoiselle."

" Remember that there are others whose permission is requisite."

" Others?—whom? where?" asked Galitzin, with genuine surprise.•

" At home in Britain."

" Ah, the little cock-boat of an island, where people jostle each other at every step; bah! you may never see it, till we visit it together after this foolish war against Russia is over, and peace proclaimed."

All this was becoming unpleasantly plain, she was to be coerced, perhaps; so she said haughtily " I am weary of all this—obey me, Monseigneur le Prince, if you please, and leave me."

" I am more used to command than to obey,"

he replied, while seating himself with perfect deliberation.

"Yes, your serfs, and soldiers, who are little better; but you have no right to command me."

"That we shall see," said he, laughing, for her grand airs amused rather than piqued him.

"Come," said she, giving him her hand, which he kissed tenderly; "do not let us quarrel; I fully believe that at heart you are a gallant soldier, and—"

"One you could love?" he added, with his moustachio close to her ear.

"Nay," she replied, shrinking, "my husband —pardon me, must be younger, and have fewer lines—"

"These are Circassian sabre cuts! You will not have me then?"

"On a fortnight's acquaintance? it is impossible."

"Am I to suppose then," he asked, in a low and concentrated tone, "that you love another?"

"Perhaps," said she, with a provoking smile.

"You dare to say this to me?"

"Who are you that dare to question me?"

"*Who* am I?" he exclaimed, in a loud and imperious voice, while he started to his feet, and Gwenny became dismayed. "Mademoiselle, is this a vaudeville we are acting?"

"Prince," said she, "the conversation is again becoming unpleasant. In accepting the offer with which you honour me, I should be guilty of dishonesty to you, to myself, and the world at large."

" I don't understand all this. Please to explain ?"

" To accept you, I ought to love you."

" Well, I suppose so—if not now, at least by and by," said he, leisurely, and playing with the tassels of his sash.

" But what if I love another ?"

" Again that hint ! Who *is* this other ?"

" I have not said that I do ; I merely said *if.*"

" Well ?"

" Then I could not marry you, and what is more, I *wont,*" she added, suddenly losing all patience, and beating the floor with her foot, while her eyes sparkled with resentment. " Set me free from this horrid place ; send me to Balaclava to my aunt and friends—send Horace too."

" Oh, the devil ! Ramhornoff, eh ? Perhaps you prefer the society of this dilettanti young countryman of yours to mine ?"

" I have not said so," replied Gwenny, feeling herself on dangerous ground.

" Ah ; we shall know each other better by and by."

" With you, Prince, this alleged love is caprice ; to me it may be fate—destruction !"

" I know that I am your senior in years—not much though ; but when better acquainted you shall find no disparity in our tastes, or temper; and if you entrust me with your future happiness, you shall never have cause to repent of becoming the Princess Galitzin."

" Never, but *once*," thought Gwenny.

Again the high-spirited little beauty was exasperated by his confident mode of annoying her; and when Galitzin saw the bright flash of the usually soft dark eye, the quivering of the cherry-like nether lip of her exquisitely cut mouth, and the curve of the proud nostril, he knew that he had nothing to hope from her concession or complaisance. He could win her, but by force or fraud only; and by one or other he was resolved she should be won. She was his prisoner, and he would take time to consider the matter well.

" You are very haughty and coy, Mademoiselle," said he, giving her one of his darkest glances, while he took his flat green foraging cap and jerked his sabre under his arm; " but if I find that your friend—your cousin, or whatever he is—this Capitan Ramhornoff, stands in my way, or will not use his persuasive powers for me, I may dispose of him as I did that fellow Chesters, who robbed me in Paris !"

And with these threatening words, which he closed by some tremendous Russian oath, he left her.

She remembered Rebecca and the Templar in the castle of Torquilstone, and ever so many more heroines and melodramatic situations with which the contents of the box that came quarterly from Mudie's to Willowdean had stored her mind; but she gathered no comfort therefrom, or from the conviction that there are "greater novels in real life than in stories."

They were all perilous scrapes—unpleasant, desperate, and so forth, and in this age of gas, steam, and electricity, absurd and unsuited to the case; yet a spice of her Indian breeding came at times to her mind, and she felt, that if sorely pushed and she had a weapon, Major-General the Prince Galitzin, Colonel of the Tambrov Infantry, &c., might stand a very fair chance of having a hole punched in his skin.

CHAPTER XIX.

SOON after the last interview we have narrated, Galitzin went in search of Horace Ramornie. He had not to seek for him long, as the nearest sentinel pointed to where he lay on the grassy slope of the glacis outside the fortress, listlessly, to all appearance, though sunk in sad and exciting thoughts.

However, he started up and, as policy required, saluted courteously the person who now approached him, but whom he loathed with an intensity that words cannot pourtray.

"Still contemplating the road towards Sebastopol, and the sea?" said Galitzin, with a smiling countenance, and in French. "Ma foi! you'll not require to make a sketch of it, as it must be graven pretty well in your mind by this time. Will you have a cigar?" he added, proffering a handsome silver case, which had been found in the pocket of one of our Guards' officers on the field of Inkerman.

Cigars were luxuries of which Horace had long
been deprived, and as declining might have
savoured of insult or open dislike, he accepted
one and lit it at that of the Prince, the two
looking into each other's eyes pretty much
as we have all seen John Mildmay and Captain Hawkesly do in the latter's " Office in the
City."

" So you are anxious to be free, eh ?" said the
Prince.

"Why taunt me by a question so tantalizing?"

" I do not taunt you; far from it.   Well, I
don't care if I afford you an opportunity for
being so."

" How ?" asked Horace, whose heart, while
longing for liberty, revolted at the idea of having
it without that of Gwenny Wedderburn also
being secured.   " I have given my parole, and
your Government——"

" Know nothing about you as yet.   I have
troubled Mentschicoff with no reports for some
time back.   I can make you a close prisoner
and yet afford you a chance of escaping.   A
horse—yes; even a Tartar pony, would soon take
you to Balaclava."

" But what means this sudden change in your
views, and where are your fears that I might
detail the strength, the defences, and so forth, of
Yaila.   What am I expected to do in return for
this favour?" asked Horace, suspiciously.

" You are right to ask, for, as I always say, it is a nothing for nothing world ours.   Well, you may do much for me."

" Explain, Monseigneur le Prince—pray ?"

There was a pause; the usual detestable glitter came into the cold and half-closed eyes of Galitzin, and Horace rightly surmised, that if he were once out of Yaila with the aforesaid Tartar horse, he should find—whatever favour he granted or service he performed—the road beset a few versts from the place, and that then he would be shot down without mercy or despatched as a close prisoner to Yekaterinoslav ; for he knew that his present companion was capable of any act of treachery, however dark, or base, or cruel.

"As your friend Chesters would have said——"

" Excuse me ; he was no friend of mine," said Horace.

" Your brother officer then ?"

"Nor that either," replied Ramornie, haughtily. " The unfortunate fellow had only local rank in the Turkish Contingent, and had to quit Her Britannic Majesty's service for malpractice with cards."

" Well, your fair friend Mademoiselle Wedderburn and I have had one or two long conversations together, and as Chesters would have said, in his sporting *parlance*, she is a stake I mean to enter for.   You understand me ?"

" You mean to make her a proposal of marriage ?" said Horace, with a smile that in spite of himself was somewhat ghastly.

" Precisely ; and I wish you to use your influence—that is, if you possess any, with her, for me. Tell her that if she will marry me without any fuss or absurd resistance, I shall open up to her a life of wealth and brilliance at St. Petersburg or Moscow—she can have her choice—at Baden-Baden, and elsewhere, such as she cannot conceive and could not have in England—that land of fog, of exclusiveness, and insular prejudices, where everything foreign is deemed ridiculous and judged by the standard of Pall-Mall or the Old Bailey—your *Times* and your *Punch*. I know all about it ; I have been in London, and was there too long for my own profit."

He certainly had not been there for the profit of others, as " this interesting foreigner" had been required more than once at Bow Street, and was not forthcoming.

" Have you not already proposed ?" asked Horace, quietly tipping the ashes off his cigar.

" Yes ; but she can't make up her mind. It will after all be, at best, a poor style of ingrafting, as the gardeners say ; yet the blood of the Tegoborskis may be perpetuated through my pretty one for all that."

Ramornie made a violent effort to control his rising rage, an exhibition of which would have been useless, and only serving to spoil all, so he said, simply—

"You are unfortunately older than the lady, Monseigneur le Prince."

"Yes—perhaps—somewhat."

"Old enough indeed to be——"

"Don't say, her father—that would sound unpleasant. I know that with a disparity of some twenty years between us, I shall have all the ordinary commonplaces of well-bred life said of me on *that* score, and perhaps to me, for the girl seems wonderfully cool and self-possessed. She will talk to you, no doubt, of the brevity of our acquaintance, our partial ignorance of each other's tastes and dispositions—perhaps also ask whether I have not already a Princess elsewhere," he continued, with his ugly smile. "Seek to explain all this away, and to assure her that, save with me, she has no hope of ever returning to England. But though there be a difference in our years, as I am a Russian Prince, it is not necessary that I should sue for this girl in a tone of humility."

"I do not quite comprehend all this," said Horace, bewildered by stifled rage.

"Well, I mean that my renewed offer is not to be blended with an apology—by you at least."

"Have you no humane or religious scruples in this matter?" asked the other, scarcely knowing what to say.

"Oh, as to religion," replied Galitzin, laughing heartily, "you don't think surely that I am particular to a shade about the tenets of the *raskolniki*," for so dissenters from the Russian Greek Church are named.

" But she, I hope, has some scruples."

" She has told you so ?—perhaps you are more in her confidence than I am ?" said Galitzin, with flashing eyes, for his suspicions were ever prompt to kindle.

" If I am *less*, why seek my aid or influence? Besides, you forget, Prince Galitzin, that we are almost cousins ;" and as Horace spoke, he remembered again how Lady Wedderburn used to resent the term or idea ; but there it proved most useful, for his hearer felt and knew from a Russian point of view that ties of blood barred both love and marriage within the fourth degree ; and so his suspicion lulled again, and he said—

" Monsieur le Capitaine, let us seek to understand each other."

" You are sure you love her ?" asked Horace in desperation, to gain time and to think.

" I always dreaded a regular love fit as I dread the evil-eye or the devil ; but how could any man escape with her, she is so perilously handsome? She has a lovely hand, and an irreproachable foot and ankle. What a ravishing peep I had of them yesterday as she stepped out of the pony-phaeton. Say to her, that I implore her to come to terms for her own sake, as she is perhaps far from safe where she is."

" Terms—safe," stammered Horace.

" I have put her in Norina's charge—under Madame Tegoborski's care, I should say. Now, Madame has been absurd enough to conceive a mad fancy for me. Of course, I am a Prince and Major-General, while Tegoborski is only a Pulkovnick, and has been a serf (though a relation of mine), who joined the army with one half his head shaved, for so we always mark our recruits to prevent them from running away. But she threatens me——"

" Who—Madame ?"

" Yes," said Galitzin, lowering his voice, and glancing furtively about, as if he feared being overheard, " she threatens me, and might, for all I know, poison the poor girl ; women are terribly vindictive, and that would never do, with such a fine fortune as she has. Will you expatiate on all these dangers as an old friend ? and if your advice weighs well with her, you shall have a horse for Balaclava to-morrow."

" But if it does not weigh with her ? For I may fail as an adviser, if you as a lover have failed already."

" Then I shall try other means. I shall take her away with me alone to Bagtche Serai or elsewhere for a few days, and that will compromise her honour in her own eyes and those of the world, if the world cares about the matter. She will then see the absolute necessity of a

marriage with me. Beautiful as she is, I may
frankly tell you that it is not her person I value
so much as her purse. I have rank, but I must
have roubles as well. I want money, and this
war will soon be over now; yet in my time I
have drunk and gambled away serfs enough to be
the population of a moderate city."

"But even this last scheme may fail; and
what will you do then?"

"Resort to *force!*" hissed the other through
his teeth, and thinking that to say more might
lessen the strength of his instructions, which did not
seem very clear to Horace Ramornie, he lifted his
forage cap, bowed, and withdrew, leaving his
listener rooted to the spot in a storm of indignation, rage, and natural fear, though not for himself.

"Scoundrel!—open and confessed as such!"
muttered Horace, as he watched the figure of
Galitzin disappear through the arched gate of the
fort; "you little know your man, or the task
you have set him! Anyway, I will have an
interview with my beloved Gwenny, and may con-
cert something with her. But what can that something be? Have I not thought of all, in vain,
before? Oh, God aid us!" he added, looking
upward with clasped hands.

It was dreadful to contemplate the idea, or
rather the fact of his idolized and highly-bred
Gwenny being in the hands of a man who could

conceive such schemes, and canvass them openly! In the course of a few minutes, what had he not hinted, suggested, or threatened; and now there was a new terror, in the jealousy of Madame Tegoborski!

He threw himself on the cool grass, to think; but how often had he thought in vain before! And there he lay scheming—considering this doubt and that probability, this plot and that plan, till his brain grew giddy with intense perplexity.

The Russians he knew to be corrupt and ready to take bribes; but he was not the master of a copper kopec. And in yonder Tartar village there was no one whom he could intrust with a message to Balaclava, or whose aid he could seek. He looked wistfully at its flat-roofed cottages, almost buried among the green leaves and golden apples of luxuriant fruit-trees. He turned to the fertile valley that led towards the Black Sea, which blended with the sky in sunny haze, and then to the dark pine forest, that clothed the southern slope of the Tchatr Dagh, the marble cliffs of which seemed to vibrate in the rays of light. But no shelter for her could be found there.

Did his parole bind him still, at a conjuncture so terrible? He feared that it did.

He felt powerless, and weaker by having Gwenny's fate linked there with his own; and he envied now the stupid and monotonous existence he had enjoyed before her peril, and anxiety for her safety, came to torture and agitate his mind.

Great was the horror of sitting there help-lessly unarmed, penniless, and powerless; and not knowing what an hour — yea, a minute, might bring forth!

Anyway he would see Gwenny at once; and, with a prayer for inspiration and guidance in his heart and on his lips, he passed the *tête du pont* and entered the fortress.

CHAPTER XX.

IF, even to save Gwenny Wedderburn, he broke his parole of honour and escaped, he knew that he should inevitably forfeit, at home, his position as an officer and gentleman for ever. If he withdrew it, that would be simply a warning to Galitzin that he meant flight, if he could achieve it; and to preclude that, he should be made a close prisoner, helpless to assist her, and probably sent away to the rear, like poor Newnham, who, exasperated by the brutality of his capture, had declined to give his parole at all in any way.

It was, every way, a horrible dilemma!

Could he by any means communicate with the officer commanding the nearest allied forces or outpost? He had by this time, however, ascertained that the Russian troops in Tchorgoun —that place which had proved so fatal to his destiny—the nearest point to Yaila, were very insignificant in number, though their position

15—2

was strong, and connected with that held by their army along the whole line of heights between the Tchernaya and the Belbek.

He inquired for the Hospoza (*i.e.*, Madame) Tegoborski, of the pretty Karaïte Jewess, who had, doubtless, received her full instructions beforehand, as she at once ushered him into the bare and chilly chamber which we have already described as the "drawing-room" of the Pulkovnick's lady, to which some additional ornaments had been added, in the shape of gildings washed up by the sea from the Ernescleugh yacht; and there Gwenny was seated alone, busy with some needlework, which she tossed aside, and hastened to receive him with a bright and tender smile.

They were alone, and were instantly hand in hand!

Ramornie could perceive with concern, that since he had last seen her, there was a change in her face, the result, doubtless, of the "worry" occasioned her by the absurd and obtrusive attentions of Galitzin and her separation from himself, when they had so much to say, so much to ask and to tell each other. She had become thinner; her large, dark, and finely-lidded eyes —usually so full of brilliant expression and emotional changes—looked dull and weary, till they caught some vivacity from his.

"Oh, Horace darling, how have you been enabled to visit me? I feared they were about to keep us for ever apart, those horrid people! Do they fear our conspiring, or what? Four whole days, Horace, and I have not even seen you!" she exclaimed.

"I have come at the suit of a lover of yours," said Ramornie, with a smile on his lip, but a stern expression in his eyes.

"Who? that odious Galitzin?" asked Gwenny, laughing.

"The same, darling. But this is no laughing matter for us—for you especially. I dare not tell you all that man has ventured to hint, and commissioned me to say."

"Well, I don't want to hear it. Pet Horace, sit beside me here, and talk to me; we shall speak of each other and not of him—the Russian toad!" and drawing closer to her lover, she nestled her sweet face in his neck; and yielding to the charm of the situation, they forgot all about Galitzin, and sat dreaming in silence, or talking of Willowdean and the Lammermuirs, of St. Abb's Head, and the wild sea shore, of scenes and places far away, of past times, their earlier emotions as they stole into their hearts, and of much more on which their *listener*—for they had one—could not enter.

"And Galitzin has been making you proposals?" said Horace, suddenly coming back to their present predicament.

"Yes, frequently; ridiculous, is it not?"

" And how do you receive them ?"

" I laugh; but there are times when I become angry.   He is an absurd old creature; I loathe the sight of him, with his strange cruel smile, and sincerely hope that he wont come here to pester me with any more of his solemn, hard and deliberate love making, that has not one atom of softness or tenderness in it."

"Could I get pistols and an opportunity, I should blow the brains out of this middle-aged Russian cupid !" said Ramornie, in a low voice of concentrated passion.

" Oh fie, Horace; he cannot mean anything serious," said Gwenny, her eyes dilating with surprise at his quiet vehemence.

" Ah, my love, you know not the man or all he is capable of; unfortunately, I do. My letters informed you how infamously poor Cyril suffered at the hands of a Russian officer whom he was succouring, when we stormed the heights of the Alma."

" Yes."

" Well, that Russian officer, so wantonly ready with his pistol; the notorious spy so often found in our camp at Varna, and even in the trenches at Sebastopol—he who could so wel act the part of a Frenchman, is Ivan Tegoborski the Prince Galitzin; but—but—did you not hear a noise ?"

" Oh what is all this you tell me ?   A noise !

no, I heard only the beating of my heart, dear, dear Horace."

"Poor little heart! It may have much to make it palpitate yet. If I had only some money for bribery. Oh, if Heaven would only give me the means———"

"Money, Horace, is the root of all evil, says the proverb; and but for the reputation of wealth, I should not be troubled by this Galitzin."

"True; but money is also the root of all good; for none can be done without it."

"How well he speaks English."

"Ah, and French too—the *mouchard !*"

To a certain extent he explained to her, the views, the wishes, but not the ulterior threats of Galitzin in case of her non-compliance; his tender love and her natural delicacy, made him shrink nervously from a hint so odious; but she fully understood and recognised all the danger of the position occupied by Horace and herself though she could not quite understand the difficulties.

On Horace Ramornie had rested all her hopes for weeks past; they must meet some time alone, she had thought, when they should have a careful conference and sudden flight together; though the chief obstacle seemed the want of money, a vehicle and horses. But when he set the latter wants before her, with the moral and military

obligations enforced by his parole, the penalties
of breaking it, the Cossacks' eyes that seemed
constantly to watch him, and the chance of his
transmission to Yekaterinoslav, her heart, so full
of hope and fond anticipations, seemed to die
within her.

And little thinking that they were watched by
jealous eyes, they would frequently clasp each
other's hands by the instinct of sudden affection,
and sit thus for precious minutes in silence, gazing
into each other's eyes that were full of tenderness
and light.

When they did speak, it was fortunately in
a tone that was low, and heard by themselves only.

"Good Heavens, darling!" said Gwenny, suddenly, "it cannot be that in this time of civilization and progress, as the newspapers call it,
we have got into a scrape of the Middle Ages—
an adventure worthy of some old castle on the
Rhine!"

"I am afraid it looks deuced like it, Gwenny,"
replied Ramornie: "but oh, if the Allies would
only take an airing this way, and knock the whole
place to pieces! One Lancaster gun should do
it in two hours! but they devote all their
energies to Sebastopol, and never think of the
petty outposts."

"And oh, Horace, if this man should take me
away from you?" suggested Gwenny, in a really
piteous tone.

" I would kill him in front of his men !" was the husky reply.

" And be bayonetted or shot instantly ?"

" I ran those risks daily with the Fusileers, for no reason that I could see, Gwenny ; but Heaven alone knows what you and I shall do !"

" And I had formed such a nice plan for our escape !" said she, mournfully.

" You, my pet love ?"

" Yes," she sobbed.

" And your plan, darling, what was it ?"

" Simply this—it involved a little horse stealing, however."

" Go on, Gwenny, go on."

" You know that Madame Tegoborski often drives me out, without any attendants, in her little phaeton, which is drawn by two Tartar ponies ; and I thought that if you could contrive to meet us, unexpectedly as it were, a mile or so from this place, you might simply assume her seat and whip, and we should drive off together ! She would soon give an alarm, of course——"

" Nay, I should tie the old hag hand and foot to a tree——"

" But oh, Horace, wolves might come !"

" Let them," said Ramornie, savagely. " Yours *is* an admirable plan, and I am astonished that it never occurred to me before ; but it is woman's wit, and you have such a clever little head, darling. Then," he added, with a sigh, " there is my—parole !"

" Oh that weary parole !" exclaimed the girl, as her head and spirit drooped again ; " it destroys our only plan, our sole remaining hope ! This very evening we are to drive so far as the pine wood, on the road between those two great mountains with the fantastic names."

" The Tchatr Dagh and the Demirdji."

" Yes ; you know it, then !"

" I have seen the wood from the gate ; it lies some versts beyond the distance I am permitted to go from the glacis of Yaila."

" Can you *not* break this promise ?" she whispered, imploringly, with her hands on his shoulders and her bright eyes looking imploringly into his.

" No, it is impossible ; an officer's word once given thus is irrevocable !"

" Then I am in despair ! Oh, Horace, Horace, what is to become of us ? What is to become of me ?" exclaimed the girl, in a passion of grief, as she flung herself upon his breast and clung to him, so full of her own and their mutual sorrow that she was quite unconscious of the door having opened and shut, and that Galitzin stood behind her with lowering, inquiring, and malevolent eye.

" You here, Monseigneur le Prince ?" exclaimed Ramornie, indignantly, and not without alarm, as he tenderly deposited the half-fainting girl upon a sofa.

"Oui, ma foi!" replied the pale, unhealthy-looking Russian, with his detestable grin; "and what then? I was simply adopting the privilege of Le Diable Boiteux, and peeping in here."

"And, doubtless, you have overheard all?"

"I am sorry to say that I have not."

"How so?" asked Ramornic, greatly relieved.

"You spoke rather too low for that; but I can guess its interesting nature, as I have *overseen* all."

"Silence, for Heaven's sake, Prince Galitzin; do you not see that this young lady is almost fainting, and cannot even speak?"

"Ah, indeed!" replied Galitzin, scornfully. "'Silence adorns the sex,' says Sophocles; perhaps silence, seclusion, and sal-volatile, together with a glass of kimmel will be advantageous here. Have the goodness to see to this, Madame," he added, as the wife of Tegoborski entered, and with an exhibition of considerable agitation, the exact source of which it might be difficult to discover, seated herself by the side of Gwenny, while Galitzin, saying to Horace, "Follow me, Monsieur le Capitaine," led him into an adjoining roc....

" Now, Monsieur, I must speak plainly," said Galitzin; " we understand each other perfectly, I believe. How often have I made love, as people say, St. Ivan Veliki alone knows; but this time I am in earnest—I have an additional incentive, and shall not be crossed by you. A turn of the wheel of fortune has thrown a golden opportunity in my way, and I shall not be such a fool, such an utter Asiatic, as to neglect it !"

Galitzin paused and breathed hard; for opposition to his wishes had begun to pique and inflame him; while, on the other hand, young Ramornie, proud and fiery by nature, inspired by all the genuine emotions of a gentleman and a free-born Briton, felt as if on the verge of madness, and yet had to be most guarded in all he said and did.

" Beware, Prince Galitzin," said he, as the drowning will cling to straws; " in proposing to marry this orphan girl, you, a foreigner, a stranger, one of a different religion———"

" Bah! you said all this before. What care I, though she were a Hindoo ?"

" You promise yourself a month's amusement during the *ennui* of Yaila, forgetting that to her it may be the destruction of a life."

" You mistake me, my would-be Mentor. I promise myself the enjoyment of a fine fortune when the cannon of Cronstadt and the Kremlin announce peace to Europe. But by Heaven I don't understand you, or this tone of insolent advice that you have ventured to adopt!"

"She has trustees—if you understand what I say—and you may not be able to get at her fortune without *their* consent, even if you married her to-morrow," said Ramornie, quietly.

Galitzin seemed to be transported with rage by this new suggestion, for he felt the too probable truth of it.

"Vassili blajennoi!" he exclaimed; "this to me? Say as much more, and I would not give a copper kopec for your life!"

A bitter smile escaped Ramornie on hearing the pious invocation of a saint blended with a threat of violence against himself. For this man had no religion or real veneration for holy things; yet in his superstition or adherence to outward forms and to traditions of the Russian Greek Church, he would as soon have thought of pistolling himself as of sitting down to his dinner of green borsch and stuffed carrots without first bowing to the *eikon;* or of killing and eating one of the countless pigeons, which at Yaila, as in every other Russian edifice are to be seen clustering in clouds over the roofs, belfries, and cupolas, and sitting in long rows like cornices along the eaves; for it is pre-eminently the holy bird of the Muscovites. On fast days he would not even look on butter or cream; but in place thereof, used plenty of oil for his *ouka*, or fish-soup of sterlet, or salmon cutlets, pleasantly boiled in vinegar and flour *à la Russe*.

"Do you actually threaten me, a prisoner, an unarmed man?" asked Ramornie, after a pause.

"I do; so beware, Monsieur le Capitaine, of what you are about. It is not known, I am almost sure, to the Allies that you are in our hands, as you stumbled among us amid the snow on that dark night march to Tchorgoun; and as yet I have never sent in your name to Prince Mentschicoff. Hence I might, without the slightest risk of being questioned, make as short work with you as I did with that fellow Chesters when on the march to this place. If inclined to be more merciful I could send you inland with a note—a mere note of a few words would do—which would ensure your safe transmission to Tobolsk or Irkutsk. The mines there, if not favourable for the lungs are admirable for the development of the muscles, and you have been getting fleshy in idleness, though having a thirty-two pound shot at one's heels is apt to cure one of all taste for dancing. Now we understand each other, I think?"

"And this is said to me within fifty miles of the British camp before Sebastopol?" said Horace, with crimsoned brow and sparkling eyes.

"Well, perhaps a few versts more or less."

"Such threats are alike ungenerous and outrageous!"

"I could hang you by the wrists from a tree with a cannon ball for one toe to rest on; and how should you like forty-eight hours of that without food or water?"

Even that threat was more than sufficient for Horace Ramornie!

"Enough," thought he; "I shall be at the pine wood this evening, and trust to Heaven and my own wit for the rest!"

"Take care how you trifle with me," said Galitzin, almost as if he understood or read what was passing in the mind of Ramornie. "You will wish yourselves among the graves of Inkerman, rather than here, if you bring my jealous vengeance on you."

Horace could scarcely understand to what all these threats tended, but drawing himself up and eyeing the Russian sternly he said, proudly and haughtily—

"I demand, Prince Galitzin, that you shall remember that I am a British officer on parole of honour, and in no way subject to you."

"A British officer—bah! I do not forget it. In three days we shall have a convoy proceeding to Yckaterinoslav. Prepare, Monsieur, to accompany it with your hands tied again to the mane of a Tartar pony if you are not marched there on foot!"

And, as Galitzin said this, he bowed and left the room.

"This again more than ever renders my parole null and void," said Horace, in a low and concentrated voice, in which passion and satisfaction were curiously mingled; "three days? now for Gwenny's plan of escape, and this very night too! Blessed be Heaven, that Muscovite rascal did not overhear her!"

CHAPTER XXI.

THERE was something of fierce elation in the mind of Horace Ramornie when he found himself alone ! On giving his parole of honour that he should not go beyond a mile from the glacis of Yaila, it had been, of course, distinctly understood that his life must be respected, and his personal liberty too. Now the former had been threatened and the latter also ! The compact had thus been vitiated by the Russian Major-General, so Ramornie was free—free to escape when or how he could !

He knew the contingencies; that he was certain of a degrading captivity if three days hence found him in Yaila, and certain of death if he fled from it and was *retaken.* Anyway, to free Gwendoleyne Wedderburn was worth risking all for, and that evening he resolved the attempt should be made, minus though he was of arms, money, or a guide. He would simply adopt the plan she had conceived; he should meet her and Madame Tegoborski at the pine wood; assume that lady's place in her vehicle and drive off, testing the speed and muscle of the Tartar ponies to the utmost, and the whole matter seemed very easy, provided no interruption occurred by the way.

The plan was only a little horse-stealing from the enemy, and under the high pressure of the circumstances quite justifiable.

About an hour before the projected design, he left Yaila by the barrier-gate, as if for one of his usual solitary strolls, but not without an increased beating of the heart, as he fancied that every stolid-looking Russian sentinel in his flat cap and hideous long clay-coloured coat, eyed him more keenly than was their wont; but this was the mere result of feverish anxiety; and he proceeded slowly along the ancient road that led towards the Black Sea, whose waters he could see in the distance, rippling in golden light at the end of a valley. He frequently paused and seated himself on the grass, again to walk slowly on, thanking his stars that the two Cossacks, Alexis and Ivan—their surnames he never knew—who had been wont to hover, singly or together, so mysteriously on his steps, or within his range of vision, were now absent, having been sent with poor Bob Newnham to Yekaterinoslav.

Sometimes he clasped his hands and looked

upward. Was it possible that this night might see him a free man; free, with Gwenny by his side, and within a few miles of the British outposts?

There are few places where one has been resident even for months only that they do not quit with regret; but Ramornie simply loathed Yaila in all its features; the green painted cannon, each with a red cross on its breech, the brick-faced curtains and embrasures, constructed by Baron Todleben, who had also patched up the old towers of the days of Justinian and of the Genoese; the angular visages and tattered uniforms of the garrison; the green slopes around and the flat outline of that "table mountain," the Tchatr Dagh towering over all!

Heaven be thanked, he was about to see the last of them—and with Gwenny, too!

He had read of, and fancied many a melodramatic incident; but scarcely conceived that in sober, civilized life such things could come to pass as had happened to him; yet our Afghan war, a few years before, and the subsequent Indian Mutiny, were alike full of terrible situations, painful and harrowing escapes and perils, undergone by lovers and friends, by husbands, wives and their children! But who can foresee the sudden and startling contingencies that are consequent to a state of warfare, especially in wild and lawless lands?

16—2

And now, beyond all their present peril, as he threw himself on the green sward to think and ponder, Horace Ramornie looked forward fondly to spending his future life—a happy home life—with Gwenny, as to a promised land, where they should talk over the *present* with wonder, and even with pleasure!

He was now on the skirts of the pine wood, and being quite concealed by some little caper bushes, could watch the road that led to the quaint old fort on the green hill slope. The crimson light of the setting sun was glowing redly on the gnarled stems and twisted branches of the old forest. All were shining as if with flame, and the birds were singing their last notes loudly amid the wiry foliage. The dry cones were dropping, and the field mice were scampering homeward to their holes under the long rank grass.

Beyond the green Babugan mountains, he could see that the road wound through a shady dell, where the tall white poplar, the dwarf almond and the pretty linden tree grew together in luxuriance; and by that valley he knew they should have to pass in their flight, after he had possessed himself of Madame's equipage. But how was he to dispose of *her*, and prevent her giving an alarm that in ten or twenty minutes would ensure pursuit!

His eyes seldom turned from the gate of Yaila,

as every instant he expected to see the shaggy
ponies appear; and how, if Galitzin took it into
his head to accompany them, as he frequently
did? He always rode with a pair of revolver
pistols in his holsters. As this idea occurred to
him, Ramornie looked round for a suitable stone
—but hark! There was a sound of hoofs and
accoutrements in the valley, and very soon a detachment of Russian cavalry, some fifty files or
so, came along at an easy trot, evidently from
Tchorgoun.

They were all Don Cossacks, with grey fur
caps and huge red moustaches, the twisted points
of which were quite visible from behind; their
blue tunics worn halfway to the knee were girt
by scarlet sashes, and their wide loose trowsers
were thrust into their coarse jack-boots; and so
defiling past, and chanting a rude hoarse ditty,
they passed through the archway and entered
Yaila, greatly to the mortification of Horace;
for thus Galitzin had at hand swift, ready and
instant means of an effectual pursuit and recap-
ture in every direction!

Another hour, to the anxious lurker a seeming
eternity, passed away, and the sun, which had
been above the marble summit of the Tchatr
Dagh when he first came forth, had sunk behind
it now, and his ruddy golden rays spread sky-
ward among the light floating clouds, like the
spokes of a fiery wheel, while the singular out-

lines of the Dimirdji and Babugan mountains rose in purple and black against the red evening clouds. The odour of the wild thyme came pleasantly on the passing wind. The monotonous plash of the water sounded ceaselessly from an ancient stone fountain near—a relic of the Genoese; but though athirst with feverish anxiety Ramornie never drew near it. Close by too were purple grapes, ripe figs, soft peaches and blooming nectarines all growing wild; but he heeded nothing. He ever turned his eyes to Yaila; but the archway appeared only as a black spot in the walls, from whence nothing seemed to issue.

A knowledge that the place where he lay was beyond his paroled distance, added to his anxiety, so his suspense, dread and doubt, amounted ere long to actual pangs of bodily pain. Was she ill?

"Oh what *can* have happened—why do not they come?" he continued to exclaim from time to time, long after there could be any chance of the Hospoza Tegoborski taking her evening drive.

Suddenly the boom of a cannon gave him a species of electric shock. A thin white puff was curling upward from the northern bastion of the fort, and he saw the Russian Cross streaming out upon the wind, which brought the sound of drums towards him. Had the garrison received information of an attack? What had happened?

He had not a moment to lose now, for even if he saw the columns in red pouring through yonder valley, he must return and report himself to the officer of the main guard—more than all he must return to where *she* was, and on entering, he found the whole garrison under arms, in two quarter-distance columns, with bayonets fixed, and a fresh supply of ammunition being rapidly distributed from casks which were strewed in front of each regiment.

His heart beat high and happily. An attack, he though, *must* be expected; and those Don Cossacks were the forewarners of it!

"Do you expect an attack, Monsieur le Colonel?" he inquired in French, of old Tego-borski, as that personage limped past. "I presume those Cossacks brought the intelligence?"

"They have brought none, Monsieur," said Galitzin, ere the Pulkovnick could reply. "They are simply the convoy I spoke of, *en route* to Yekaterinoslav, whither you shall go with them in two days now," he added, with his old smile. He had a peculiarly malevolent pleasure in hurting the feelings of others—of the young especially; for as his own youth was long past, he hated that joyous period of life in any one else.

There was no attack, and the night passed away in peace; but the whole of this sudden alarm and preparation, which thus baffled the

plans and hopes of the prisoner, were the mere
result of Russian superstition.

The *bell* of the chapel had fallen from its rusty
hook, decayed by time and exposure. This was
deemed by the garrison in general, and by
Galitzin in particular, as significant of some dire
and impending calamity, because the Muscovites
deem all bells as something sacred, and when in
the preceding February, a great bell fell in the
tower of St. Ivan Veliki at Moscow, crashing
through four floors in succession and killing all
the inmates, it was regarded as the omen of some
much greater calamity to Russia; thus, on the
day after, news reached the Holy City of the
death of the Emperor Nicholas !

Ramornie cursed, in his heart, the wretched
superstition by which his only plan had been
marred. But one evening now remained to the
fugitives, and if it proved one of rain ; if Madame
Tegoborski had the vapours, or was indisposed to
drive, the noon of the third day would see him
once more under escort, and accompanying those
red-whiskered Don Cossacks, towards the Isthmus
of Perecop.

Though Ramornie knew it not, and feared the
worst from the plump fair Muscovite with the
sleepy eyes, large hands, and snowy arms, she
was neither an enemy to him or Gwenny.

With all a woman's quickness, she had seen
and discovered their secret — that they were

lovers. From a quiet point, through an eyelet-hole, she had overlooked their recent interview which Galitzin had so unceremoniously interrupted, and she became earnestly desirous of succouring them for their sakes, and somewhat for her own, that she might remove from Yaila and the Prince's vicinity, a rival so wealthy, beautiful, and young; though she had a wholesome terror of him on one hand, and a little, perhaps, of her spouse, the Pulkovnick, on the other.

Lack of language—for she knew only her native Russ and a few stray words of German—rendered the difficulty of arrangements and explanations very great; but, most luckily for the conspiring trio, it chanced that at this very time there had arrived with the detachment of Don Cossacks, an officer of rank, deputed by the Princes Mentschicoff and Gortchakoff to inspect the garrison with its stores and report thereon, as both Kertch and Yenekale had been captured by the Allies, and several discrepancies had been detected in the nominal returns of Prince Galitzin; in short, the "men of straw," in his muster-rolls had been suspected, and the pressure of affairs in Sebastopol rendered further trifling impossible. So His Excellency had his hands full.

One interview with Gwenny and Ramornie sufficed to complete their new plan. Madame's arrangements were simply and speedily made for their flight, and, in a burst of gratitude, he threw his arms around her ample waist and kissed her on both cheeks—a process to which, as he was a more than usually good-looking young fellow, she submitted with the best grace in the world.

Taking advantage of the confusion—almost consternation—and occupation of Galitzin and the Pulkovnick, Madame arranged that she should ride her saddle-horse, a fine and active Tartar one, next evening to the pine wood, accompanied by Gwenny on foot. There Ramornie was to precede them, and lie *perdue* as before. She would mount the lady, and he must lead her bridle ; their way should lie through the Baider Pass, some fifty English miles to Balaclava. They must travel in the night, conceal themselves by day, and trust for the rest to God, she added, bowing to the *eikon* in the corner.

She did more : knowing the great risk run by Ramornie if he travelled in a red coat (or the remains of that which once had been a *red* coat) she supplied him with a Russian caftan of canvas, girt in the approved fashion with a rope. Still he was without arms, and he donned this ungraceful attire, never reflecting the while, that if he appeared thus within range of a sentinel of the Allies, he might be shot ere he could answer a single inquiry.

All succeeded beyond even their fondest anticipations; and when, next evening, the shadow of the Tchatr Dagh fell on the pine wood and the valley of the wild almond and linden trees, Madame Tegoborski was lingering on the Yaila road, looking back, and kissing her hand to the retiring figures of Ramornie and Gwenny, whose newly acquired horse he led by the bridle, as they descended into a steep dark glen that they believed was ultimately to lead them to the Pass of Baider.

CHAPTER XXII.

"Fifty miles, and for you afoot! Oh, Horace, Horace, I can never be so selfish as to ride!" said Gwenny, in sorrow and commiseration.

"It is only two very long days' marches, Gwenny," he replied, cheerfully, for his heart was beating happily, and he paused a moment to look back, to caress, and kiss the gloveless hand that held the reins. "The last portion we may take leisurely," he added, "for then we shall be near old Colin Campbell's headquarters. What a trump Madame Tegoborski has proved after all! and yesterday I actually thought of tying her neck and heels with a vine trailer. Thank Heaven, the darkness comes on fast!"

But unfortunately, with the darkness there set in a dense white mist from the Euxine. It came rolling in masses along the grassy valleys and up the rocky mountain slopes, and ere long amid it and the obscurity of the night, all trace of the narrow roadway became as completely lost as if it lay under the snow drifts of that night of the fatal march to Tchorgoun!

Muffled in a warm cloak of the Hospoza's, Gwenny did not feel cold; but her heart, like that of her companion, became filled with natural anxiety. They had completely lost the path now, and the horse, though led carefully by the bridle, stumbled and lost its footing every moment amid loose stones, caper-bushes, and stunted turpentine trees, on what seemed to be the slope of a mountain side. At last Horace paused in utter irresolution, and the bead drops rolled from his temples. For aught he knew to the contrary, he and his companion might be proceeding straight to, and not from, Yaila, and daybreak might find them in sight of it!

Lost together on a dark mountain side in Crim Tartary, how strange it seemed to Horace, the knowledge that the girl whose soft and plaintive accents came to his ear from time to time, was the same bright and light-hearted Gwenny from whom he had parted in the drawing-room at Willowdean when he left home to rejoin the Fusileers, and dared only press her hand—she whom he had clasped to his breast so tenderly before. Yet so it was, and truth is stranger than fiction!

The livelong night they wandered slowly and irresolutely there, and Gwenny was sinking with fatigue, while Horace, preternaturally wakeful and nervous, listened for every passing sound; but none came on the soft breeze that sighed through the waste so lightly as scarcely to roll the mist before it.   No Russian drum or bugle, no sound of alarm-bell, and no Cossack halloo were then "piercing the night's dull ear."   All was still, and when grey dawn began to break and the mists to exhale upward, the wanderers found themselves yet somewhere about the base of the Tchatr Dagh, and near a Tartar farm or large cottage.   Horace swept the landscape with a keen and haggard eye; no vestige of Yaila, with its four green domes, and no sign of scouting horseman could be seen.   All the land seemed woody and fertile, but desolate of people.   That was well and his mind was relieved; but his delicate companion required instant rest and succour, so he approached the dwelling of the Tartar with mingled hope and anxiety.

Early abroad, the Tartar farmer met them at his door, and surveyed them with doubt and mistrust.   He was a keen-eyed and sharp-featured man, of middle age; his shaggy, black brows seeming to mingle with the fur of his sable cap. His features were not of the flat Mongolian type, but were pleasing, regular, and fair.   He saw that the lady was weary, and required alike food and rest; and when she had dismounted, he led them into a room, softly carpeted and cushioned, with a fireplace in it—a mark of civilization—

and a little table, some twelve inches high, in the centre, whereon he placed milk, curds, and cake ; but Ramornie made Gwenny imbibe some Crimskoi wine from a crystal cup ; and being without money, she pressed upon the Tartar's acceptance one of the rings she wore, and he took it, glancing with undisguised covetousness at those which still remained upon her slender fingers.

To his alarm, Horace discovered that they were not far from the hated Yaila. In fact, amid the mist, they had been describing a kind of circle in their peregrinations overnight, at the base of the Tchatr Dagh, and even the southern end of the pine wood was still visible !

Gwenny seemed already so worn and weary, after all she had undergone of late, that Ramornie had great fear of her ability to keep in her saddle till she could reach Balaclava ; and he conceived the idea of getting succour from thence halfway.

In a strange Polyglot kind of language, partly Turkish, English, and Italian, eked out by signs, he continued to make the Tartar understand that he wished a message taken to Balaclava, and his host averring that he had a swift horse, offered to bear it, if paid therefor ; so all Gwenny's rings were to be his on the answer coming back, and she freely proffered them.

" May Allah increase the glory and the substance of my lord!" whined the Tartar; "and mayest thou never know hunger," he added to Gwenny, giving her the kindest wish of his people. "Drink," he continued, giving her more of the effervescing and refreshing Crimskoi; "it is pure as the holy well of Mecca:" but she closed her eyes wearily, as if to sleep, and Ramornie surveyed her with apprehension and solicitude, as she lay back on the cushioned divan, listless and pale.

Oh, if she should become seriously ill on his hands in that wild and out-of-the-way place—so near Yaila, too!

He asked for writing materials. None were to be had; but a quill plucked from a hen's wing, a little gunpowder mixed with water, and a fly-leaf, torn from an old Koran, thus making the message more sacred, supplied the three requisites: and Ramornie wrote a note to be delivered to the officer commanding the nearest out-post, imploring that succour should be sent along the road that led by the seashore from Balaclava towards Alushta; and adding, that if an attack on Yaila were projected, there were only in the place two Russian battalions, of four companies each, and twenty pieces of cannon, the heaviest being 32-pounders. He added his name, rank, and regiment; and requested the Tartar to depart at once, showing him all the rings that glittered on the white hands of 'the now sleeping girl, as the reward of his speed and fidelity.

"May Allah increase the glory——" began the Tartar again.

"There, now," interrupted Horace, "that will do. Be off; spare not spur nor whip, and the reader of my message may also reward you for our sake."

"Speech is silver; silence is gold," replied the Tartar, sententiously, and a few minutes after saw him mounted and away at a gallop southward, by the road towards the headquarters of Sir Colin Campbell; and again hope began to dawn in the breast of Ramornie.

In front of the flat-roofed farmhouse there rose a steep ridge of rocks. Up these he clambered to watch the progress of his messenger; and how great were his disgust, his disappointment, and anger, when he saw the fellow, after conceiving himself quite out of sight, ride directly *north*, and disappear past the edge of the old pine wood, along the road direct for Yaila.

He had gone to betray them to Galitzin —to that Galitzin, whose scouting Cossacks might even now be within a few versts of them!

Inspired anew by anxiety and alarm, he hastened to rouse poor weary Gwendoleyne, and replacing her in the saddle, after appropriating a sabre that hung on the wall, they set forth in search of another place of rest or refuge.

A narrow, winding, and sombre path, over-hung by oaks and beeches, soon hid the house of the traitor from the fugitives. The morning was clear now, and the sun shone cheerily along the mighty green slopes and impending cliffs of the Tchatr Dagh. After a time the trees were left behind, and rocks alone bordered the way. Ramornie looked for a place of shelter, and if possible, of repose, for his delicate companion, for Gwenny was sinking fast. At length, his keen and haggard eyes detected a dark fissure in the red marble cliffs. He hobbled the horse in a little thicket of turpentine trees, and half lead-ing, half carrying his tender charge, he conveyed her into what ultimately proved to be a cave, strewed apparently with dry chips and white branches of trees; but these, in fact, were human bones—the relics of a Tartar slaughter—for they were in the famous grotto of Foul Kouba.

He placed her on a ledge of rock, and wrapping her cloak about her, kissed her on both eyelids, and bade her sleep if she could, while he would wait and watch. Looking forth from the mouth of this uncouth hiding-place, he could discern about six miles distant the four white towers of Yaila shining in the sun; but no

figures were stirring in the open ground between.

Again he turned to watch his sleeping charge,
and then what were his horror and dismay to
see the figure of an armed Cossack, who had
evidently issued from the inner part of their
retreat, bending over her with curiosity, pistol in
hand.

CHAPTER XXIII.

ROBBED and stripped by plunderers, in short by the Cossacks of the escort, of their money, jewels, and even their outer garments, Lady Wedderburn and Lady Ernescleugh reached Balaclava, the neat white houses of which were now almost hidden by more recent erections of huts, stores, and so forth, even as its slender population of Arnaouts had become lost amid the overwhelming numbers of its new occupants, the Highland Brigade, Rifles, and other British soldiers of all arms and uniforms; and in the distance their anxious eyes could see the three-tiered batteries, the green domed churches, and the lofty houses of that Sebastopol, whose name was then in the mouths of half the world.

They reached the headquarters of Sir Colin Campbell in such a plight, and in such a state of excitement, that the testy but warm-hearted old Scottish General, after telling them that it was alike impossible for them to go to the front,

or to remain in Balaclava, as deaths were occurring every hour by cholera, and that the
Sardinians at Tchorgoun had lost a thousand
men in three weeks by disease, transmitted them
without much ceremony on board a steamer,
then just starting for Scutari; and before the
poor ladies quite knew where they were, they
found her steaming out of the harbour of
Balaclava, amid all the *débris* of wreck and drift-
wood, and the festering and floating carcases of
cavalry horses which encumbered it.

There, at Scutari, they had been told by some
one, they knew not who—a staff officer apparently,
in tattered uniform, with a haversack under his
arm, and wearing a prodigious beard—they
"should get intelligence of their sons."

The boat left the vessel's side and he was
gone.

"Has Cyril been wounded again?" thought
Lady Wedderburn; but ere long, on board the
steamer, she learned all!

Poor Cyril had fallen at the head of his company, on the 8th of the preceding June, in the
memorable attack, when the great Mamelon, the
Quarries, and the White Works were stormed and
taken by the Allies. On that occasion, among
a host of others, the Master of Ernesclcugh had
been wounded and sent to Scutari, so it
was to him that Sir Colin Campbell's aid-de-
camp had referred.

Who can open the Book of Destiny, or see the slender thread, the link or chain of events, that leads to fortune or to fame—to misery or calamity ? Happy it is for us that we can never see the future !

Cyril had fallen by a ball through the chest, at the base of the Picquet House Hill, and there he lay, while the tide of his comrades swept on— lay dying and alone, under the sultry sun, while the dull mist of intense heat mingled with the smoke of the conflict, and settled down in the breathless valley, where there was no air to rend it aside; and as his blood and his life ebbed together, there seemed to come to his drowsy ear the voice of Mary Lennox, singing, and he thought himself again listening to her in the garden at Lonewoodlee.

It was the voice of a French sister of charity, at a little distance. She was chanting the *De Profundis* amid some dying Zouaves, and when her song ceased the soul of Cyril Wedderburn had passed away.

Upon the table in his hut the poor fellow had left a will, hurriedly written. Therein, after piously giving his soul to God, and his body to be buried by the finders, if he fell, he bequeathed certain sums to wounded soldiers of the Fusileers and to the widows and orphans of others who had fallen in the war. His love he left to his parents, brother, and all friends, adding that he

would die at peace and with goodwill to all
men.

And so he was found lying on his face stone
dead when the burial parties came.

Nightfall saw the handsome and gallant soldier
shovelled away, with hundreds of others, into the
trench-grave—" the vast lumber-house of death"
—and the secrets of Mary's love, and of all her
sorrows, were buried with him.

Cyril dead! Oh, could it be, thought Lady
Wedderburn, that all the objects and wishes of her
life had changed within so short a space of time?

" Oh! my Cyril, my son, my pride! and has
it ended here, and ended thus?" she wailed out
on the breast of Lady Ernescleugh, when she
read the last letter sealed for her, and left in his
hut. " Oh, where now are all my fond aspira-
tions! oh, my hope! my joy! they have ended now
in death! Oh, Cyril! why did I ever bear or nurse
you? Yet, I am enduring only what many a poor
mother has endured since this fatal war began."

And she wept long the tears of unavailing
sorrow, while her maternal heart went sadly
home, and back to the sweet days of his tender
and loving childhood, when he, who had fallen a
handsome and stately soldier, had clung to her
skirts, clambered at her knees, and nestled in
her bosom, a beautiful, a happy and smiling child
with dark eyes and golden hair; and so the loss
of her son, combined with keen and sharp anxiety

for Gwendoleyne, brought on a species of low and nervous fever, under which she lingered on for many weary weeks in Misseri's Frankish Hotel at Pera. She was not confined to bed, but lay propped on a sofa at the open window, from whence she could see the vast and glittering panorama of Stamboul and all the Golden Horn, with the three-deckers of Abdul Medjid lying at anchor, with the star and crescent flying; but nothing could rouse her. She thought ever of the dead Cyril, the lost Gwenny, and her now futile *wish*.

"Oh, wherefore should we heap up riches," she would say, "when, as the Scripture tells us, we know not who shall gather them! Oh, Juliana, dear," she added to Lady Ernescleugh, whose son was now convalescent, and was able to lounge about Pera with glazed boots and carefully parted hair, "I did not think it possible that I could have heard of my Cyril's death, though daily I knew he risked life, and yet live on as I am living. But I don't think I shall survive it long. See, my poor hair has become quite grey, and is coming out fast."

"Use cantharides, dear," lisped Lady Ernescleugh, as she lounged on a satin divan and fanned herself with a bunch of feathers in a pearl handle; "it is an excellent specific," she added, as she saw that her friend's "division" *was* becoming wider than its wont.

So the quiet, unsentimental and unenthusiastic
Robert Wedderburn, who had in his time
" spoiled more foolscap than cartridge paper,"
plodding over his books in the Temple, became
the heir of Willowdean and the old baronetcy,
the stately mansion, and the Burgh of Barony,
with all their political interests, while a grass-
covered mound at the base of the Picquet House
Hill, was all that remained to his elder brother.

CHAPTER XXIV.

THE CAVE OF FOUL KOUBA.

"A Cossack, a dog of a Cossack, by Heaven!" exclaimed Horace Ramornie, in a low voice of intense emotion, as he unsheathed the sabre with which he had provided himself at the house of the Tartar, and saw his apparent foe, a wild-looking fellow, with matted hair and cap to match, and clad in a rough shoubah, come hastily towards him.

"English, now thank God!" exclaimed the seeming Cossack, in whom Horace instantly recognised Newnham, the commander of the yacht. "May I never!" he added, turning to the sleeping girl, of whose face only the handsome mouth and set of small white teeth were visible. "By Jove! if this isn't Miss Wedderburn, and you—you in the caftan like a Ruski?"

"Captain Ramornie, of the Royal Fusileers."

"And don't you recognise me—Bob Newnham?"

"Of course I do," was the response; and they

shook hands heartily, each being intensely relieved by discovering *who* the other was; and the sound of their voices awoke the sleeper. Alarm was her first emotion, and then her natural sense of fun caused her to laugh at the odd figure cut by her old friend Newnham; for they had been great friends on board the yacht, the poor and soured Lieutenant R.N., having sunned himself for a time in the charm of her society, though he knew that the pleasure would end some day, but not so disastrously as it had come to pass.

" By Jove, Ramornie, I feel almost comfortable now and quite happy, for the idea that Miss Wedderburn was in the hands of those beastly Ruskies was maddening to me," said Newnham, when he had heard their story. " I wish I had a pipeful of tobacco or a cigar, however. I have often made both one and t'other do duty in place of fire or a tot of hot grog on a cold night-watch."

" But how did you escape and obtain these arms?"

" And this elegant costume? Well, if you guessed till your hair was grey and as long as the Atlantic cable, you never would hit on the right thing. It happened in this way. The two fellows who escorted me proceeded for, I don't know how many miles, towards Perecop, passing between Karasu Bazar and the Putrid

Sea, till one fine day, about a week ago, they made a halt on the banks of the Karasu, in a fertile and beautiful valley, covered with yellow and green tobacco fields ; and though we had gone so far, still the flat scalp of this mountain, the Tchatr Dagh, was visible at the southern horizon.   That I might share their black bread and quass they took the devilish handcuffs off me, but each had by him a sabre and loaded pistols, as a hint of what I might expect if I attempted anything unpleasant.

" The scenery was lovely, the air delightful, and the halt most welcome ; for I was weary and thirsty ; but the *dolce far niente* character of our little picnic underwent a rapid change.   It chanced that the Cossack named Ivan had planted his butt-end fairly upon a hollow place, containing a large wasps' nest.   On finding himself stung by one, he furiously discharged a pistol into the hole, and in a moment the air was black with them.   They came not alone from that hole, but from a score of others.   I sprang to my feet and bolted a little way, for in a trice the two Cossacks were covered with them, wasps and bees too, were on their faces, necks, ears, and hands.   They buried their heads in the long grass ; they roared, and raved, and rolled about in utter agony, so I resolved to lose no time in making the best of the opportunity.   I seized the cap of one, the shoubah of another, then provided myself with the arms of Ivan and the horse of Alexis, and leaving them to their sorrows rode as if the devil was after me, by the very way we had come. In fact, I rode till my horse dropped under me, and I was compelled to leave it, poor animal, to the vultures. Then I lost my way, and for days have been wandering, feeding myself on whatever I could pick up, till chance last night brought me this way, and here I am."

Newnham related his adventures so briefly and jauntily that even Gwenny could not help smiling through her tears.

"Come, Miss Wedderburn," said he, "don't have a faint heart in harbour, after having shown a brave one at sea."

"But we're not in harbour yet, Captain Newnham."

"We soon shall be, and laugh over all these things. You have had a lucky escape from that rascally Russian, and in my heart I thank God for it," said he, kindly patting her fingers with his strong brown hand. "It is a queer bunk this," he added, surveying the cave, and looking at the sunny landscape that stretched far away below its mouth or arch of rock, which seemed to form a frame for it like that of a picture; "but what are all these that strew the floor?"

"Bones," said Horace, in a low voice.

"Bones!"

"Yes, human ones. Hush!"

In this cavern a party of Genoese had been smoked to death by the Tartars (just as the French used to make a razzia among the Arabs in Algeria), and their bones are still lying there. So at this hour the tourist in the Scottish Hebrides may see in the cavern at Eigg the bones of the Macleans, who were there smoked to death in a similar fashion by the Macdonalds. This Crimean den is of vast extent ; for Monsieur Oudinet, a Frenchman, is said to have " penetrated half a day's journey into it, without reaching the end." Be that as it may, our fugitives contented themselves with lingering at the mouth thereof.

Though they had no food, the day passed rapidly ; they had all so much to say and to tell each other, and it was proposed that at nightfall Gwenny should mount again, and some progress be made towards the valley of Baidar. Balaclava could only be some thirty-seven miles distant. So, when evening came and the shadows of the Tchatr Dagh fell far across the sunlit valley, and melted away in general darkness, Newnham crept forth to scout and listen ; for mist was stealing in from the sea again.

Secure for the time, as they deemed themselves in that uncouth place of shelter and secrecy, Gwendoleyne laid her throbbing temples on the breast of Ramornie, nestling herself there, as if sure of peace and security, while he pressed his lips to her brow from time to time ; and so they remained silent, hand in hand, heart speaking to heart only, till a sound roused them.

It was Newnham creeping in to announce that "some infernal Ruskies were in motion in the valley below, as he could hear by their horses' hoofs;" doubtless a scouting party brought by the treacherous Tartar.

A low cry of alarm escaped Gwenny.

"Now do take heart, Miss Wedderburn," urged Newnham; "remember that, as some writer has it, 'no pleasure is lasting that is not dashed with a sense of danger.'"

At that moment the Tartar horse hobbled in the thicket below neighed; after a few seconds there was a response from another amid the mist below. Then came the sound of voices, and of feet, as if many men were scrambling up to the mouth of the cavern, and Horace felt his heart beating painfully and wildly, as he clutched his sabre, resolved to die hard. To do that was easy, but what of Gwenny then?

Through the gloom and obscurity of the misty night they could see the figures of the dismounted Cossacks making their way up the slope; but just as the foremost had come within twenty yards of the hiding-place there was the report of musketry on the road below, and by the flashes it became evident that an exchange of shots was taking place between the Russians and some hostile force.

The leading Cossack paused, and next moment a huge stone, hurled from the hand of Ramornie, dashed him into the mist below. His comrades lingered doubtfully in the ascent, as if they knew not whether to fall back or advance, for the firing continued to increase in the dark below, and by the distance between the flashes it seemed to have been opened by troops extended in skirmishing order, feeling their way as they slowly advanced.

Suddenly a loud and authoritative voice rang out, and once more the ascent to the cave of Foul Kouba was resumed, while a large and brilliant fireball, thrown almost into its mouth, revealed all within. Steadily it burned in the still atmosphere of the breathless night, casting a green and ghastly glare on the red marble walls and arched roof of the vast natural grotto, lighting up many a point and feature hitherto unseen in its gloomy recesses, on the wild weeds that grew in luxuriance about its entrance, on the whitened bones that strewed its floor, on the shrinking figure of the pale and terrified girl, and on her two guardians crouching, each with sabre and pistol in hand, behind a mass of rock, intent only on defending her to the last gasp and dying as hard as possible.

Steadily, we say, burned the weird and ghastly light, and the first face it fell upon was that of Galitzin. He had lost his cap in the ascent, and was clad in his light green uniform lapelled with white. He was armed with a sabre and revolver pistol.

He fired the latter thrice at Ramornie, but the balls only starred the rocks behind him, and the echoes found a hundred reverberations in the black profundity beyond. The sneering courtesy, the sleek aspect, the cold and glittering smile of Galitzin, all were gone now, and the eyes, the bearing, and the expression of the human tiger had replaced them. The man looked all instinct with ferocity and recklessness. He was haggard, ghastly, and savage, as he cast one furious and inquiring glance to where the rifles were flashing through the gloom below, and then sprang into the mouth of the rocky den with uplifted sword, to be instantly cut down by Horace; for the sharp and trenchant Damascus blade, of which he had so opportunely possessed himself, clove the truculent Muscovite to the left eye, and he fell prone at his feet, without a groan!

Another who followed him was shot by Newnham, who speedily despatched two more with his sword; and now, scared by the fall of their leader and by the increasing fire of musketry in the mist below, all who were ascending fled down the slope and disappeared, leaving the fugitives free; but one, ere he went, discharged his carbine back at random, and by this Parthian shot Ramornie had his right arm broken above the elbow.

"Vive la France !" cried a voice out of the obscurity. "Mes Zouaves, suivez-moi !"

Then, after a time, came the sound of the Scottish bagpipes, and of the shrill Zouave trumpets, sounding the advance.

"By Jove ! an attacking force at last, and not a moment too soon !" exclaimed Bob Newnham.

The tread of feet, passing double-quick along the valley below, re-echoed for a time, and occasional shots were heard and flashes seen, dying away in distance and obscurity. Newnham, to prevent Gwenny being shocked, trundled the fallen Russians down the slope; and the remainder of the night was passed in hope mingled with suspense and anxiety.

When day dawned, the white flag had disappeared from Yaila, and two of darker tints were floating over its leaden domes, doubtless the union and the tricolour; and two columns of infantry, one in red and one in blue, were encamped on the plain within a mile of Yaila.

Still the fugitives did not venture forth, though Ramornie was enduring the greatest pain in his wounded arm, and Gwenny was overwhelmed with grief about him, as she sat by his side watching his pale face, while he clenched his teeth to conceal his agony. About noon two mounted officers in French uniform came galloping back to the lurking-place to discover who had been firing from thence over-

night; and one of these proved to be Colonel
De la Fosse, who informed them that Sir Colin
Campbell, on ascertaining the exact whereabouts
of Yaila, had dispatched a regiment of his
Highland Brigade with a few guns towards it,
in conjunction with the 34th Infanterie de la
Ligne and a battalion of Zouaves sent by General
Bosquet. To this combined force the Pulkovnick
Tegoborski had surrendered without firing a
shot, and all his garrison were prisoners of war.

"Sacre tonnerre!" added the Frenchman,
"and yonder fellow lying dead on the slope is
the spy, after all—aha, *le scelerat !*"

"He is the Prince Galitzin," said Horace.

"Cut down by Captain Ramornie, and serve
him right," added Newnham.

"And you, Mademoiselle, ma douce amie,"
said the Colonel, approaching Gwenny, cap in
hand; "this is no place for you, so we shall
forward you to Balaclava in a Tartar kabitka;
and meantime I shall send the surgeon of the
Scottish regiment to dress your wounded arm,
Monsieur le Capitaine. Aha, mon brave! we
have just come in time; but by the horns of the
devil, I would rather have cut off my moustachios
than have had that pitiful Russian mouchard to
escape. And now, adieu! for I must ride back
to Yaila."

"We shall meet again, I hope, Monsieur le
Colonel?" said Ramornie, cheerfully.

" Allons ! I hope so ; all the roads in the world lead to Rome—or to Heaven. Adieu, Mademoiselle !" he added, and lifting his kepi, bowed low and hurried to where his horse awaited him. But they were fated never to see the gallant Louis De la Fosse again, as on the 8th of the following September, he fell at the head of the 34th Infanterie, at the storming of the Malakoff Tower.

CHAPTER XXV.

THEY joined Lady Wedderburn at Misseri's in Pera, and her reunion with Gwenny, was the first gleam of joy that had visited the poor woman's heart since that morning on which the stranded yacht was so foully cannonaded by the Russians.

After his wound was dressed, Horace had paid a farewell visit to his comrades at the trenches, and brought away his cousin Cyril's baggage; but the packing thereof — slight and slender though his fighting wardrobe was—proved a sorrowful task; for few mementos bring the presence of the dead so powerfully before us as garments they have worn, or the objects of their solicitude. Among other things Horace found Maltese crosses, Gozza buttons from Valetta, roseleaf bracelets full of sweet perfume from Stamboul for his mother, Gwenny, and even little Miss M'Caw; a Turkish pipe for Bob, swords from the Alma, bayonets from Inkerman, a fragment of an iron shell from the Valley of

Death for Sir John—suitable presents for every-body.

His tattered Fusileer uniform, his bruised epaulettes, his Indian medals and rusted sword were brought away by Horace. Then too his photos, little mementos of the happy home circle, each and all treasured as sacred *lares* by Cyril in that Crimean hut, and often looked at fondly and lingeringly in the long hours of the weary night, while the great guns were heard pounding away, and men were dying fast amid the frozen mud and gore of the fatal trenches.

A few letters there were, at which Horace glanced; they were in a lady's hand, and tied up with a white riband. Ramornie dared not read more than a line, for the secrets of the dead are sacred; but they were full of earnest, passionate, and girlish love, frank, tender, and adoring; for they were the few—a dozen or so—that Cyril had received in happier days from Mary Lennox.

Now both hearts were still—still for ever; and the spirit that had invoked spirit were perhaps together now, in the Shadowy Land that lies beyond human ken.

Horace placed the packet in the camp fire that burned outside the hut, and after watching the embers smoulder, resumed his sorrowful packing with one hand. These letters seemed now but as "the vague shadows of a vague existence."

" Life is made up of bitternesses, Gwenny," said Lady Wedderburn, as she caressed the girl's head in her bosom, " and I have brought a few upon myself and you ; but ere long we shall be safe at home. Yet Cyril, my darling Cyril, can never be restored to me, and it seems so cruel and strange that I shall never see him more !" And as she spoke all her mother's heart—and God knoweth how great a heart that is—went forth for the dead son. " My poor Cyril !" she resumed, as she resigned her to Horace. " I cannot conceal from you, Gwenny, that I had other views and another wish concerning you ; but God hath willed it otherwise, and may you and Horace be happy !"

A few days after this saw them all " off for Old England, as fast as black diamonds and boiling water could turn the screw-propeller," to quote Bob Newnham, who was left behind in command of a large transport, a post procured for him by Lady Ernescleugh.

" Oh, I am so thankful !" exclaimed Gwenny, looking at the canvas as it was sheeted home to accelerate the vessel's speed.

" Thankful for what, darling ?" asked Horace; " to be free ?"

" Not that alone, but to be once more upon the sea—the great ocean ; it is like the beginning of home."

" Home, Gwenny, darling ? we are not yet

past Seraglio Point. Yet I understand your feeling."

"So do I, Miss Wedderburn," said Newnham, whose boat was alongside, and who was gazing on her admiringly. "You feel like myself; that when on blue water you are on the high road to Old England. Ah, you should be a sailor's wife!"

"Ah! but she is to be a soldier's," said Horace, "and the water is green here."

"And green water always shoals," replied Newnham; and bidding them a laughing farewell he descended the side ladder and shoved off to his transport.

Though clouded by natural regret for Cyril, the heart of Gwenny was full of happiness, and her dark eyes shone with liquid light, while all her face seemed to beam with sweetness and bright intellect as she surveyed Horace Ramornie, her future husband, and admired his perfect features, his erect air, broad chest, and lithe figure so full of strength and symmetry, all save the poor wounded arm in its scarf of black silk.

She was with him she loved and who loved her. She forgot the past and all her tears, and absolutely blushed at her own joy as the great steamer sped on its homeward path, their eyes ever seeking each other, and never, never wearying of the search.

Her glossy black hair was simply braided and girt by tiny diamond stars upon a narrow velvet band round her head, displaying the pretty ears and fine contour of her neck and throat. Her dress was black silk, trimmed with narrow white lace, and she had silver bracelets, necklet, and cross, all enamelled with black, as mourning for her cousin.

"Ah," thought Horace, as he surveyed her, while she sat on the poop twirling her parasol under the awning, "who in the world, with any idea of joy or happiness, would be a bachelor!"

But neither could say all they felt then—

> "For words are weak and hard to seek,
>   When wanted fifty-fold;
> And then if silence will not speak,
> Nor trembling lip, nor changing cheek,
>   There's nothing to be told!"

If it is difficult to describe our own happiness it becomes next to impossible to pourtray that of others. So we shall not attempt to expatiate upon the emotions of Gwenny and Ramornie; yet, like all happiness, it had its alloy, for they could not but revert to the memory of him who lay in his lone grave by the Picquet House Hill.

"I couldn't send in my papers, Gwenny, even as your rich husband, while the war lasted, but this broken arm luckily settles all for me," said Horace. "It is England and sick leave in the first place."

"With me for your nurse—and your dear little wife, Horace."

They looked back from the poop, for now they were in the Sea of Marmora. The tall cypresses of Scutari, the mosques, the domes and minarets, and all the flags of Stamboul, the city of the Sultan, had lessened in the distance, and were blending with the golden evening haze as they sped on the world of waters; and when the night came down, and the stars came out in the deep calm blue of the sky, Gwenny still sat there, with her hands clasped in those of her future husband—the realization of a young girl's dream.

THE END.

www.ingramcontent.com/pod-product-compliance
Lightning Source LLC
Chambersburg PA
CBHW030622030726
47497CB00006B/1595